Retold My

African Myths

African American Folktales

Asian Myths

Classic Myths, Volume 1

Classic Myths, Volume 2

Classic Myths, Volume 3

Mexican American Folktales

Native American Myths

Northern European Myths

World Myths

The Retold Tales® Series features novels, short story anthologies, and collections of myths and folktales.

Perfection Learning®

Consultants

Linda Goss
Norfolk, Virginia

Lorraine Hall
Charleston, West Virginia

Rosalie Kiah
Norfolk, Virginia

Retold Myths & Folktales

African American Folktales

by David Haynes

Perfection Learning®

Writer
David Haynes

Senior Editor
Marsha James

Editor
Lisa Morlock

**Cover and Inside
Ilustration**
Don Tate II

Book Design
Kay Ewald

For information contact
Perfection Learning® Corporation
1000 North Second Avenue, P.O. Box 500
Logan, Iowa 51546-0500
Phone: 1-800-831-4190 • Fax: 1-800-543-2745
perfectionlearning.com

Paperback ISBN 0-7891-1893-9
Cover Craft® ISBN 0-7807-6574-5

9 10 11 12 13 14 PP 10 09 08 07 06 05

ABOUT THE AUTHOR

David Haynes has spent fifteen years teaching middle-level students in urban schools, mainly in Saint Paul, Minnesota. He has participated on planning teams for numerous school reform efforts, including the Longfellow Humanities Magnet School and the Saturn School of Tomorrow, where he served as an associate teacher of humanities.

Haynes has also been affiliated with the National Board for Professional Teaching Standards as a member of the Adolescence/Generalist Committee. More recently, Haynes has been the Teacher-in-Residence at the National Board's Washington, D.C., office. In this capacity, he worked with many of the nation's finest educators to develop teaching standards in the fields of social studies,

vocational education, early childhood education, and for teachers of students whose first language is not English.

Haynes' first novel, *Right by My Side,* was published by New Rivers Press in 1993. It was an American Library Association Best Book for Young Adults Award and was nominated for a Minnesota Book Award. *Somebody Else's Momma* was published by Milkweed Editions in April 1995 and in paperback by Harvest Books in 1996. Also published in early 1996 were *Heathens* by New Rivers Press and *Live at Five* by Milkweed. The West Seventh Wildcats, a series for young adults that includes *Business as Usual* and *The Gumma Wars,* was published in 1996.

Haynes has had other short works published in *City Pages, Stiller's Pond, Other Voices,* and *Glimmer Train.*

These works have also been recorded for the National Public Radio series Selected Shorts.

Haynes has received several literary awards. He was a recipient of the Jerome Foundation's Literature Travel and Study Grant in 1989 and a Minnesota State Arts Board Fellowship in 1995. He is also the winner of the 1992 and 1995 Minnesota Voices Project.

ABOUT THE ARTIST

Don Tate II is a Des Moines, Iowa, native working as a freelance designer and illustrator. He specializes in publications for children and education.

Don does extensive research to make his art authentic, yet unique. He likes to explore various artistic styles and mediums. Over the past few years, Don has discovered the computer to be a valuable and powerful illustration tool. After drawing his sketches, he scans them into the computer to refine them with color, detail, and definition.

Currently, Don lives in Des Moines. When not working, he spends his time with his family and surfing the Internet.

TABLE
OF CONTENTS

WELCOME TO THE RETOLD AFRICAN AMERICAN FOLKTALES

I have been a lover of stories since I was a very young child. Even today, there is nothing I enjoy more than having someone read to me or tell me a story. I like stories that are surprising or funny and stories that cause me to open my mouth and gasp. I like stories that make me squint my eyes and declare that it just can't be true. And I even like stories that are scary enough to keep me awake all night. So when I was asked to write this book, I jumped at the chance. I just hoped that I could find some stories that were as wonderful as those I had always loved hearing.

Setting out to do the research for this book, I wasn't sure what I would find. I knew that there were lots of African American folktales in the world, but I couldn't have told you one from memory. I had very mixed feelings about these stories too. When I was growing up, there was a cartoon movie I saw called *The Song of the South*. It had stories told by a character named Uncle Remus. And though some of the stories were pretty good, the movie didn't always portray African American people very well. So I intentionally forgot some of the stories I knew.

Then the most amazing thing happened to me as I was doing research. I began to read the work of people who collected African American folktales. Suddenly, I came across a treasure trove of stories that I had never heard. I fell in love with each and every one of them, and I thought what a shame it was that they were lost. These tales should be as well known to people as "The Old Woman in the Shoe" or "The Three Little Pigs." I think these stories are much more fun and interesting than all of those!

I hope that you have as much fun reading these stories as I did finding and retelling them. In turn, I hope you will share them with friends and families. I want their power and their beauty to be shared with children everywhere. But most of all, I don't want them to disappear again!

African Slave Trade Routes

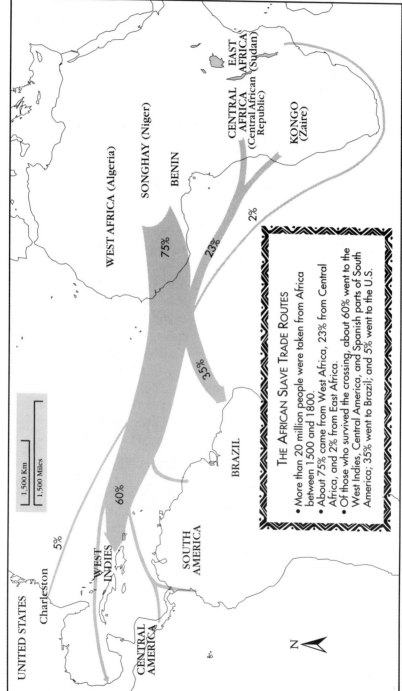

THE AFRICAN SLAVE TRADE ROUTES

- More than 20 million people were taken from Africa between 1500 and 1800.
- About 75% came from West Africa, 23% from Central Africa, and 2% from East Africa.
- Of those who survived the crossing, about 60% went to the West Indies, Central America, and Spanish parts of South America; 35% went to Brazil; and 5% went to the U.S.

1,500 Km
1,500 Miles

UNITED STATES
Charleston
5%

WEST INDIES
60%

CENTRAL AMERICA

SOUTH AMERICA

BRAZIL
35%

WEST AFRICA (Algeria)
75%

SONGHAY (Niger)
BENIN
23%

CENTRAL AFRICA (Central African Republic)
2%

EAST AFRICA (Sudan)

KONGO (Zaire)

N

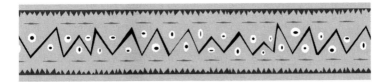

FRIENDSHIP

How the Dog Got Tame

The Poor Man and the Snake

Playing Possum

Having friends is one of the most important basic human needs. Friends make your life enjoyable and complete. Knowing that others care about you shows that you're a worthwhile, important person.

Ask people all over the world to name the most important qualities in a friend and they'll likely give similar responses: honesty, dependability, and trust. These seem to be universal characteristics of a true friend.

The characters in the following stories learn that making a friend and being a friend are not simple tasks. In each tale, a character is betrayed by someone he or she calls a friend.

HOW THE DOG GOT TAME

VOCABULARY PREVIEW

The following words appear in the story. Review the list and get to know the words before you read the story.

bellowed—shouted; yelled
cowered—cringed; hunched
lean—thin; bony
measly—small; poor
quake—tremble; shake
ravenous—greedy; piggish
retreat—withdrawal; escape
scampered—raced; hurried
scare (up)—find; search for
smugly—proudly; vainly
soothed—relieved; relaxed
survey—look over; examine
timidly—bashfully; fearfully

Main Characters

Mr. Dog—friend of Mr. Man
Mr. Fox—Mr. Dog's jealous friend
Mr. Man—protective property owner
wife—kind woman

In this story, Mr. Dog loses one friend and gains another. But maybe this trade-off wasn't such a good idea.

HOW THE DOG GOT TAME

Dogs have pretty much always enjoyed lying around and sleeping. They have also been fond of scratching, stretching, and taking advantage of a patch of warm sunlight. Nowadays, of course, most dogs like nothing better than lying comfortably at the feet of a human. But life wasn't always this way for dogs. They used to spend their time much like the rest of the animals. They often romped through the woods trying to **scare up** a meal whenever and wherever they could.

Now, this was not a horrible way to live. In fact, it was quite fun most of the time. Mr. Dog got to spend time with Raccoon, Wolf, Fox, and a lot of the other wild fellows. They'd have a good old time roaming the woods. They were looking for trouble as much as they were looking for a meal.

This would have lasted for a long time had it not been for one spring day at the end of a particularly hard winter. Mr. Dog found he and his family were rather **lean** and worn from the **measly** living they had eked out during the winter. Some of the other animals had better ways to survive the cold. For example, Mr. Bear loaded up on food in the fall while the pickings were still good. He got himself nice and fat and then slept all winter. He wasn't seen again until the first signs of spring showed in the trees and rushing water of the creek.

But the dog ran with a different crowd. He and his friends were out and about, trying to keep their families fed. It was a hard life, and this spring the dog and his family were so thin that their ribs showed. Even their coats had lost all shine and faded to the dullest of browns and grays. This situation could not continue.

About this time, Mr. Dog came across his friend Mr. Fox. They compared notes about how their winter had been.

"Hard, hard, hard," said the dog. "We're always cold, and we're always hungry. I don't reckon we can put up with much more of this."

"Well, we're all scrambling these days," said Mr. Fox. "And cold! But you know what I think? I think the answer lies over there with Mr. Man."

"Mr. Man!" cried Mr. Dog. "How do you figure?"

"Have you ever seen Mr. Man's house?" asked Mr. Fox. Mr. Dog admitted that he hadn't. His kind had always been told to steer clear of Mr. Man. So he couldn't say as he'd had any direct experience with the likes of him.

"Why, they have those bright red fire sticks that keep the whole place warm. Even on the coldest day, they can close the door and get cozy."

"Is that a fact?" said the dog. And he thought to himself that he just might see about going by this Mr. Man's house. He'd like to check into "borrowing" a couple of fire sticks himself. He talked it over with Mr. Fox, and the two of them decided to try to get some of Mr. Man's warmth.

They came up with a plan. Both would sneak up to the house in the shadow of night, figuring they wouldn't be seen in the darkness. Plus, everyone knows it's easier to "borrow" when it's dark.

When the two got to the house, they couldn't see into the high window. After each jumped as high as he could, Mr. Fox came up with a plan.

"Hey, I've got an idea," he said. "You lean over, and I'll stand on your back."

"Why do you get to be on the top?" asked Mr. Dog.

"I'm the lighter and the quicker of the two of us," said Mr. Fox. "Why, if Mr. Man sees us, who knows what he'll do. I can duck out of his view much faster than you."

That explanation was enough for Mr. Dog. He leaned over, and Mr. Fox climbed up. "Almost high enough. Can you give me a little boost?"

Mr. Dog stood on his tippy toes and arched his back.

"Almost. A little hiiiigher, a little hii—"

Mr. Dog couldn't strain anymore. Boom! Kerplunk! Both fell down, knocking against the house as they hit the ground.

The next instant, the door to the house flew open, and there the man stood.

Mr. Dog looked around. He was all alone—Mr. Fox had made an escape. "Fox was right," he said to himself. "He is the faster of the two of us."

"What do you want here?" Mr. Man **bellowed**.

Mr. Dog **cowered**. He dropped close to the ground and tucked his tail between his legs. A shiver ran down his whole body. This was the scariest voice he'd ever heard. He was so scared that he couldn't even speak. Mr. Fox hid in the nearby shadows.

"I said, what do you want?" the man repeated. In the quietest voice Mr. Dog could muster, he whispered that he wanted nothing. And, though he wanted to run away right at that very moment, he continued to lie low to the ground and **quake**.

"What is it?" a softer voice asked. "What's the problem here?"

Mr. Dog saw the voice was coming from someone very much like Mr. Man. He figured that she must be the female companion who lived in the house.

"Oh, look," the woman cried. "Why, the poor thing is nothing but skin and bones. Look, he's shivering from the cold. Bring him inside so he can warm up."

And with that, the dog was led inside. Then they seated him right in front of the warm fire. Soon he felt comfortable and warm.

"Ahh!" sighed the dog. This was the best experience of his life. To top it off, the soft hand of Mr. Man or his wife would occasionally run across his sore back. This **soothed** his tired muscles. Even better, platters of delicious food were laid at his feet. He gobbled them up in fast and **ravenous** bites. Neither the man nor his wife cared how quickly he ate. There was no need to store food for later because there always seemed to be plenty more.

Soon Mr. Fox began to worry that something had happened to his friend. So he crept to the door and scratched at it **timidly.** Mr. Dog immediately recognized his friend's signal and called back to him with a few short yaps.

"What is it, boy?" asked the man while he cautiously opened the door. Mr. Fox **scampered** away. All Mr. Man saw was the flash of a tail go into the trees. This was good for Mr. Fox, because he'd stolen a thing or two over the years from Mr. Man's outbuildings. And today he wasn't in any mood to be caught.

"You're a good watchman, aren't you, friend?" said Mr. Man. Then he passed the dog a fresh bone from the evening meal. The dog smiled and wagged his bushy tail. This was the life a dog could get used to!

And it turned out the dog had a number of other skills that the man needed as well. He was good at keeping all the cows herded together in the fields. He could point to where old Mr. Pheasant was hiding in the brush. And he was generally just a good old guy to have around.

In a short time, Mr. Dog made up his mind to stay, and Mr. Man made up his mind to keep the dog around. Eventually, Mr. Dog gathered the rest of his family and found places for them with the other men in the area. It was a good deal, and they all enjoyed having homes.

There was one loose end, however, and that was Mr. Fox. Mr. Fox was a jealous sort of fellow and did not like the fact that his friend had the easy life and he didn't.

He decided that if Mr. Dog had it in him to get hooked up with the man, then he could do it too. So, as big as life, he paraded up to Mr. Man's house and knocked on the door. Mr. Fox was prepared to offer some services of his own.

Now, Mr. Dog immediately realized that Mr. Fox had a plan. And he wasn't too crazy about someone cutting in on his good thing. So he raised a huge fuss, with all kinds of barking and carrying on.

"Good boy!" said the man as he got out his rifle and shot at the fox. Mr. Fox quickly ran off in **retreat**. The man had no love of foxes, with their too-sharp smiles and their sneaky ways. Besides, he had a perfectly fine new friend already. There was no room for another.

Life was good for Mr. Dog, and his struggles seemed to be over. Then one day Mr. Dog was out wandering along the man's fence line. Suddenly he came upon Mr. Fox, who was out for an afternoon stroll.

"You're a dirty one, you know that, Dog? There's plenty to share, but you cut me out like I was nothing to you."

"God bless the child who's got his own," replied Mr. Dog **smugly.** Then he trotted away to **survey** the rest of the land, eat a bottomless plate of food, and nap in front of a cozy fire.

To this day, Mr. Dog and Mr. Fox have been at war. But such is the way of life. Nothing ruins a friendship faster than when one has success and the other doesn't.

INSIGHTS

These days many of us turn to books for information, ideas, and entertainment. But there was a time in this country when African American people were unable to do so. Tradition and, in some cases, laws throughout the South made it a crime to teach slaves how to read. Even so, stories and storytelling became an important part of life for African Americans.

During slavery, family and friends would gather to hear a good story after a hard day's work. Stories were often repeated and, just like the popular songs of today, people had their favorites. Some stories were requested again and again. Being thought of as a good storyteller was a high honor.

In the African cultures from which many of these people came, storytelling was a long-established tradition. African American lore can be traced to centuries long ago when people might have shared myths and folktales.

To the African slaves, storytelling was a form of entertainment. But stories served several other important functions as well. They were a way of educating children about the community. Older people passed along their knowledge about how to get along in the world and how to be safe. Perhaps most important, stories served as a way to preserve history. They were a way for the community to remember important events. At community celebrations or festivals, people would gather around a storyteller called a *griot*. This practice served as a way of honoring the past and as a way of giving people a strong sense of cultural identity.

Today storytelling is having something of a rebirth. Storytellers are invited to libraries, bookstores, and community centers. In some cities, there are theaters devoted exclusively to storytelling. Many storytellers have formed clubs and organizations to share their art. The National Association of Black Storytellers is dedicated to sharing, preserving, and promoting ancient stories.

THE POOR MAN AND THE SNAKE

VOCABULARY PREVIEW

The following words appear in the story. Review the list and get to know the words before you read the story.

abiding—faithful; standing by
awe—fear and wonder
bountiful—generous; excessive
despaired—cursed; troubled
exposed—bared; uncovered
felling—cutting down; leveling
frail—delicate; weak
harvested—collected; gathered
inquiry—questioning; investigation
mourned—grieved; suffered a loved one's death
ominous—threatening; frightening
persistently—firmly; stubbornly
petulant—grouchy; ill-humored
trinkets—toys; keepsakes

Main Characters

poor man—hard worker
snake—generous benefactor
wife—spouse of poor man

The poor man's friendship with the snake brings good fortune to the man and his wife. But the poor man forgets that it's bad luck to talk about good luck.

THE POOR MAN AND THE SNAKE

A long time ago, a poor old man lived in the oldest part of the forest. He and his family lived where the trees were tall and the springs ran deep and sweet. Their house was small and made of shingles and logs. The poor man was a very good man. He and his family lived quite happily and in peace. Their only problem was that they had almost nothing. Many days they had no bread crumbs to spare. Often they **despaired** of never having enough, let alone extra.

The good man worked hard from sunrise to sunset to provide for the people he loved. He worked in the woods, harvesting trees that were ready to come down. After a hard day of **felling** timber, he would saw up the logs and branches into firewood or shingles. Then he'd haul them to the market and sell them for some coins or a few loaves of bread. It was exhausting work, and some days he was lucky to be able to sell anything at all.

One day the man was working a piece of land near the swamp. Many of the old tree roots had gotten soggy from too much water. The trees were turning black and needed to be **harvested** soon. Behind him, he heard an **ominous** hissing. He turned to find a snake staring him in the eye. It was the largest snake he'd seen in his life. In fear, he jumped back and raised his ax to strike the snake down.

"Do not be afraid!" hissed the snake. "Lower your ax, good friend. I bear you no ill will."

The farmer dropped his ax and looked at the marvelous creature with **awe**. The shiny snake coiled upon itself so that its body resembled a pyramid. It was covered with black scales that, like crystal, seemed to reflect every other color as well.

"What do you want here?" the poor man stammered.

The snake lowered his head and looked the man over. "I have been watching you," he said. "You are here in the forest working hard every day. Do you not ever take a rest?"

"A rest? Brother, what I would give for a day of rest. I work hard because I must. As it is, it takes every hour of light for me to earn enough to put food on the table. But that's all right. It's for the ones I love."

"You are a good man, indeed," said the snake. "It would be my pleasure to assist you. But first, will you make me one promise?"

"Of course, brother snake," the man said. This was the first time anyone had offered to help him at all. "Anything for a friend."

"You must promise to never tell your wife where you received this gift. If you do, you will die poor and alone in the woods." And with that, the snake puffed himself up and blew two gold coins out of his mouth.

The poor man's eyes were dazzled by the sparkling coins. They shone in the sunlight that drifted through the forest trees. "On my honor, brother snake. Not a word will pass my lips."

"Use your gift wisely, friend," said the snake. He slithered away into the swamp, wishing the poor man a good evening. The snake vowed to return again the next afternoon.

That night the poor man returned to his log and shingle house as usual. Only this time, he was weighted down with gifts for the people he loved. He had toys, sweets, and a lovely new scarf for his wife. At supper they feasted on a cake with bright frosting and sugary roses.

After seeing the children to bed, his wife woke the poor man. He had dozed off in front of the fire, as he often did after a long day in the woods.

"I love my present, dear husband," she said. "But I'm afraid I must ask you where you got all the money."

"I work hard, woman," he said in a **petulant** voice, hoping to put his wife off the subject. His wife, however, was much smarter than that. She had been married to this man for many years. And she had a way of knowing when her husband had something to hide. So she continued her **inquiry** down a different path.

"You are a good man. I know how much you do for us. You must have had tremendously good luck today in the forest."

"Don't you know, my good wife, that it is bad luck to talk about good luck?" He asked this with a sly smile. Then he gave his wife a kiss on the cheek, and she knew to let the subject rest until another day.

The next day, in the same swampy part of the woods, the snake appeared once more and gave the poor man two more gold coins. Then the snake praised him for his hard work and for keeping his promise. Again, the poor man arrived home with special **trinkets** and wonderful surprises. And again that night his wife was full of curiosity and questions.

"Another day of good fortune in the woods," she commented. She was rocking beside her husband in the comfortable chair that he had carved for her.

"Another day of hard work and another day to be happy to be alive," was all her husband would say. He closed his eyes wearily, and she left him to get his rest.

Each day for a week the snake appeared in the same part of the forest, and each day he left the poor man with two gold coins. Each night after dinner, the man would bless his family with more **bountiful** gifts. His wife would sit beside her husband and **persistently** ask after his secret. Her patience finally wore through.

"Enough!" she cried, sweeping before her husband in a new dress he had bought her just that day. "I'll have no more of this. If my husband is a thief, I'll have none of his ill-gotten gain. This must end!"

"But, dear wife," protested the poor man, who as days went by was becoming less and less poor. "I assure you this good fortune comes to us honestly. You think so little of me as to call me a thief!"

"I don't know what to think," she wept. "I just know that times are bad and money is hard to come by. In just these few days, you have brought us a small fortune. I'm afraid."

"There's nothing to fear," said the poor man, gathering his wife into his arms. She felt small and **frail** to him there. He remembered that she was the thing he loved most in the world and the thing he would least like to harm. He could not bear to see her in pain. "I have something to tell you," he said. He then proceeded to reveal the secret of the black snake with the mouth full of gold coins.

Now, to a mother raising small children deep in the forest, a snake is no friend. She had chased many away from the babies' cradles over the years. She had come to hate them with a deep, **abiding** passion.

The next morning she prepared her husband for his day in the woods. She handed him a special lunch that she had prepared just for this day.

"You work so hard for us," she said to him.

He smiled and finished his coffee. Then he bundled his coat around him on his way out the door. "Name me one man who doesn't work hard," he said.

"That snake," she said. "I'll bet he is swollen up with coins. I bet there are enough coins in that beast to set us up in style for the rest of our lives." Her eyes were fierce and fixed on all the things such wealth would do for her husband and her children and herself.

"He has been good to me," was all her husband would say.

"When you see him today, take your ax and cut off his head. You must do it for us."

Her husband walked away into the woods without giving his wife an answer. It was true the snake probably held enough money inside to ransom a king.[1] It was also true that he had been kind and a good friend. How could he hurt someone who had acted this way?

He worried about his wife's request and worked until his muscles got sore. At the usual time, his friend the snake appeared. Unlike the days before, today he spit out only one coin.

"Is that all?" asked the poor man.

The snake did not reply.

"I asked you a question," said the poor man. "Usually you bring me two coins, and today there is only one."

The snake sighed his usual long hiss. "You are full of confusion today, good friend. Perhaps I shall see you tomorrow. Perhaps not." With that, the snake made to slither away, but the poor man was enraged. How dare his friend speak to him this way.

"Come back here!" he called, and he raised his ax to strike the snake. Just then his feet caught in the **exposed** roots of a tree he was chopping down, and he tumbled forward. The ax slipped and chopped deep into his leg.

---

[1] The saying "to ransom a king" typically means to have a lot of money.

"Here I am," said the snake. "What do you want?"

"Help me," the poor man said. He was hurt and was losing blood fast. Plus, he was deep in the woods, far from home and family.

"Help you? I have been helping you for days. I have just given you another coin. I will see you tomorrow."

"Please!" cried the poor man. "I am dying!"

The snake laughed a hissing laugh. "And whose fault is that? Who told his wife a secret he promised not to tell? Who broke a promise? Who raised an ax in anger? Good-bye, foolish person."

The snake slithered away, leaving the poor man to die alone in the woods. His last gold coin sank away into the muck of the swamp. Eventually, the man's wife and children found his body. They cried and **mourned** their loss. And for many long years, their lives were harder and more full of pain and sorrow than can be imagined.

A sad story indeed, but this is what comes to those who break promises to their friends.

INSIGHTS

Most black people in the United States can trace their ancestry back to Africa. Many of the first black Americans who arrived in this country were slaves. They were forced to travel across the ocean on overcrowded slave ships. The treatment of the captured Africans was so cruel and inhumane that many died or committed suicide during the trip. Those who survived often arrived with little more than their lives. But each also had a language and culture that survived within him or her. Each had a set of beliefs and ways of doing things.

The slaveholders often tried to extinguish the native African languages and traditions. For example, men and women who spoke anything other than English were punished. Slaveholders also insisted that the slaves give up their beliefs for the religion of the area. That religion was usually Christianity.

Fortunately, it's very hard to destroy people's beliefs and traditions. Many of the slaves were able to pass on some of old-world Africa to their children and grandchildren. Very often this happened in the form of stories. Many African American folktales can be traced back to societies in Africa.

Sometimes the characters or events in the story changed from the original tale. But the main idea and the situation remained the same. Changes occurred because the climate, landscape, and animals in America were very different from those in Africa. So talented storytellers adapted old tales to fit the new physical environment. However, the roots of the old stories survived and continued to pass down wisdom and beliefs that have existed for generations.

Many folktales serve the purpose of instructing listeners about community beliefs. In the tale "The Poor Man and the Snake," the storyteller is communicating important ideas about friendship, promises, and greed. While the story is entertaining by itself, it also has a lot to teach about loyalty and the way one treats friends.

PLAYING POSSUM

VOCABULARY PREVIEW

The following words appear in the story. Review the list and get to know the words before you read the story.

cur—cowardly or mean dog
feistier—more spirited; friskier
opponents—competitors; rivals; enemies
pact—agreement; promise
predilection—fondness; liking
pursued—tried for; pushed toward
shamble—walk; shuffle
taunted—teased; egged on

Main Characters

Mr. Possum—smooth talker
Mr. Raccoon—good fighter; friend of Mr. Possum

Have you ever sworn to stand by a friend—no matter what? That's exactly what Mr. Possum and Mr. Raccoon did. But their promise and their friendship was tested when Mr. Dog came along.

PLAYING POSSUM

Everyone knows what Mr. Possum does if you come across him out on a walk. That old boy will curl up and hide himself away in a ball. Some might think that a fellow would be ashamed of a habit like that, but not Mr. Possum. This ability comes in quite handy if he meets up with trouble. In addition to his **predilection** for avoiding a fight, Mr. Possum can make up a story to explain anything imaginable. Why, he could even explain the blue right out of the sky. One day, he even explained that balling-up business.

It all started back in the days when Mr. Possum used to take his afternoon walk with Raccoon. Possum and Raccoon were best buddies. More often than not, the two might be found spending the whole day together. They had been friends forever. And they'd made a **pact** to stand by each other and protect one another no matter what. Mostly they were lunch buddies and the kinds of friends who just liked to have a good talk. At about midday, they would fill up on a big lunch of ham, cabbage, and griddle cakes. Then, after a short nap, one or the other would propose a walk in the woods.

On one particular day, the friends were strolling along their usual route. They talked about the latest gossip and about how their favorite sports team, the Wolverines, was doing. It was a crisp fall afternoon, and the trees were ablaze with bright colors. The sun shone high in a crystal-blue sky. Things were just about as perfect as they could be. Until . . .

Until the neighborhood bully, Mr. Dog, came along. Mr. Dog was known throughout those parts as being trouble with a capital T. He was mean as a snake and would pick fights just for the fun of it. And because he was big and strong, he could beat most anyone. He put a good scare in the ones he didn't beat.

Well, Mr. Dog must have been itching for a fight this particular day, because he didn't even play any of his usual games. He usually **taunted** people by talking about how ugly their coats were and about how their various relatives had fleas. But today, he just barreled down the path, baring his teeth and snapping at anyone who got in his way.

What did Mr. Possum do just then? He closed his eyes, grinned, and rolled over on that path like he was back at home in the middle of his afternoon nap. He looked as though he'd died and gone to heaven right then and there.

Mr. Dog figured he'd scared that one pretty good, so he set about to do in Mr. Raccoon. What he didn't know was that Raccoon was a pretty tough customer. Raccoon had been walking these woods by himself for quite a few years. He'd taken on fiercer **opponents** than old Dog. So the two went a few rounds. The **cur** did get in a nip here and there. But by the time it was over, Raccoon had won. He was the one strutting around while Mr. Dog scooted away with his tail between his legs.

It wasn't until all the fighting was over that Mr. Possum stirred. He lay there in the underbrush looking like a pile of leaves and twigs. Raccoon looked around for him, then decided Possum must have run off when the fight started. As any one of us might be, Raccoon was disgusted with his cowardly friend. So much for the promises to be in his corner and to stand by him no matter what. When the going got tough, Possum was nowhere to be seen. So Raccoon avoided his former friend. He decided that with friends like that, he'd be better off spending his days alone.

Possum was so still that his friend Mr. Raccoon had gone on down the road without him. Mr. Possum was pleased he'd gotten through the afternoon without one scratch on his spotless coat. He wandered back home as self-satisfied as he could be.

One day, when each was out walking by himself, the two friends ran into each other. Both were passing by a cool stream deep in the woods. Mr. Raccoon tried to **shamble** on by his friend without even saying hello. However, Mr. Possum, missing his good buddy, blocked his path and **pursued** a conversation.

"Good to see you, old timer," Mr. Possum said. "I sure have missed your company."

"I don't talk to chickens," said Raccoon.

"Chickens? Who are you calling a chicken?" asked Possum.

Mr. Raccoon answered, "You know very well you were afraid of that old dog. All you did was lie down in the road and play dead at the first hint of danger."

Mr. Possum fell over with laughter. "You got it all wrong, my friend. Me? Afraid? What was there to be afraid of? I knew that if I didn't fool that old dog with my trick, you would have. I was lying there waiting for my turn to get him!"

"You expect me to believe that? You fell over before he even sniffed you."

"Which is another thing," Mr. Possum said. "You, of all people, know how ticklish I am. When that dog stuck his nasty wet nose in my side, I thought I would just about die laughing. What good is someone in a fight who's doubled over laughing? That's just how I am. Give me a good fight any day. Just don't tickle me!"

Raccoon stood there looking at his friend for a while. He bit his lip and shook his head. No, he didn't buy that story. But you know what? Possum wasn't a bad sort of fellow. He made good conversation, liked to fish on a sunny afternoon, and always knew the best and the funniest jokes. Mr. Raccoon missed having someone to hang around with. So the two of them are still friends to this day.

And to this day, you can still find Possum balled up whenever trouble comes around. Good story or not, he's avoided plenty of nasty situations and outlasted a lot of fellows **feistier** than he!

INSIGHTS

The stories in this book are called folktales. Folktales are generally thought of as stories that are part of a specific cultural tradition. These stories are part of a culture's oral tradition—meaning they are passed along from one generation to another by word of mouth rather than written down. Oral tradition includes songs, recipes, and even celebrations. For example, in many African American families, it is a tradition on New Year's Day to cook and eat black-eyed peas. It is believed that eating black-eyed peas will bring good luck. There is no written rule that tells people to do this. It is just something an elder tells a child about, and it gets passed on and on through generations.

The stories in this book are similar to stories that have been shared in black families for many years. But as times have changed, some parts of folk culture are proving to be harder to keep alive than others. When the majority of people lived in small communities and knew their neighbors well, it was easy for traditions to survive. But now many of us live in diverse communities with people who come from many different backgrounds. It's hard to keep cultural traditions alive when there isn't strong community. In addition, almost every home has a television, radio, VCR, and other forms of entertainment. So the need to entertain each other by telling stories like the ones in this book has decreased. These stories are not often shared and are not well known, even in the African American community.

As you read and enjoy the stories in *Retold African American Folktales*, you're helping to keep the cultural traditions alive and well. And if you tell these stories to someone else, you're part of the oral tradition.

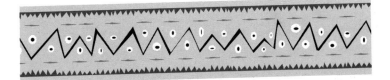

TRICKSTERS

Anansi Takes a Ride

Tug of War

Mr. Rabbit Strikes Again

High-Flying Birds

What do Anansi, Mr. Rabbit, and Ms. Nightingale have in common? All three are clever tricksters in African American tales. Characters like these have amused and entertained listeners for generations.

In addition to entertaining the audience, tales about tricksters also reveal the values of a cultural group. In addition, they teach lessons of right and wrong and what can happen when tricks go too far.

Trickster tales usually have unexpected twists and surprise endings. Often the strong, stingy, or stupid are taken in by the trickster's antics. However, the trickster can fall into the trap of another, more clever character. But even when tricksters find themselves in sticky situations, there's no need for concern. Because tricksters always bounce back—and are usually more tricky than before.

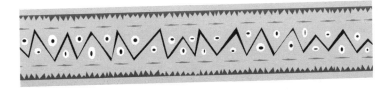

ANANSI TAKES A RIDE

VOCABULARY PREVIEW

The following words appear in the story. Review the list and get to know the words before you read the story.

envious—jealous
exhausted—worn out; tired
furious—frantic; fast
indignation—anger; resentment
sauntering—walking confidently; parading
scoundrel—bad person; rascal
stormed—angrily rushed; hurried
strolled—walked; wandered
undignified—improper; tasteless

Main Characters

Anansi—ladies' man
Tiger—handsome suitor
young lady—lovely new student

Anansi is up to no good again. This time it's Tiger who falls victim to the old trickster's trap.

ANANSI TAKES A RIDE

That troublesome old Anansi. Not only was he always going around creating problems for folks, but he was also quite the ladies' man. You know what that means—he was one of those guys who wanted all the girls to fall in love with him. He didn't care if they were smart or pretty or nice or fun to be around. And he especially didn't care if they already had boyfriends. All he cared about was making them like him. He would do anything to make that happen.

Now, it just so happens that a lovely young lady moved into a house on the next street over from Anansi. All the fellows were interested in getting to know her, but it seemed she had her eye on Tiger. Tiger was the biggest and strongest of all the guys. He wore that real pretty coat that all the girls loved. So he began dropping by and visiting with the young lady, and soon they became very good friends.

When Anansi heard about this, he became very **envious**. A young lady who had not fallen in love with him? Why, that just wouldn't do. He put on his finest clothes and his best cologne and **strolled** over to the house of the young lady in question and introduced himself.

"Afternoon, miss," he said. "I'm Anansi. I'm sure you've heard of me."

"As a matter of fact, no, I haven't," the young lady said. She was on her porch doing her math homework, so she didn't have time for any foolishness. "As you can see, I'm rather busy right now."

"I like a smart young lady," Anansi said. And he gave her his broadest smile, the one all the young ladies liked to see.

"Look, boy," the girl said to him. "I'm not impressed by your fancy clothes or your fancy cologne or your big white teeth." Actually, she was a little impressed with all those things. Like most people, she was impressed with a person who made a nice appearance. And that certainly described Anansi. Still, she decided to get rid of him.

"You're wasting your time," she said. "It just so happens I'm seeing another gentleman right now. So if you'll excuse me."

Anansi was outraged. Seeing another gentleman! He wasn't going to stand for it.

"And who might this other gentleman be?" he inquired.

The young lady laughed. "Not that it's any of your business," she told him. "But it happens to be Mr. Tiger."

Now it was Anansi's turn to laugh. "Are you kidding me?" he asked. "Mr. Tiger? Well, I can tell that *you're* new in town."

"What do you mean?" asked the young lady.

"Mr. Tiger may look nice in his fancy coat, but everyone around here knows he's nothing more than an old riding horse, carrying folks around on his back."

The young lady gasped. "I find that hard to believe," she said. She had grown fond of Tiger. However, she'd have to reevaluate him if he was so **undignified** as to haul someone around on his back.

"Don't take my word for it. You can ask him yourself," Anansi said, interrupting her thought. Then he wished the young lady a good afternoon and took off to work on the rest of his plan.

Meanwhile, Tiger got himself fixed up and came **sauntering** down the street. He had made a date earlier in the week to come by and visit the young lady. When he got to her house, they sat on the front porch as usual. But this time the girl put her textbooks between them and would hardly talk to him at all.

"What's the matter?" asked Tiger. "You seem upset this afternoon."

"It's just something somebody told me," she said.

"And what might that be?" asked Tiger.

The young lady thought about it. She didn't really like to repeat gossip, but in this case she felt it was important. She might as well get it out in the open. She didn't, after all, want to be seen around school with someone who had no class.

"A certain person told me that you were nothing more than an old draft horse[1] who rode people around on his back all day."

Tiger jumped up in **indignation**. "Who said that about me?" he roared. "I demand the name of the **scoundrel** who's spreading such rumors!"

"Well," said the girl, "if you must know, it was that Anansi fellow. And he seemed to know what he was talking about."

Tiger **stormed** from the porch. "We'll see who does the talking when I'm finished with that coward!" He raced to Anansi's house in a burst of **furious** speed.

Meanwhile, Anansi had run his body temperature up by exercising on his rowing machine. Then he had covered himself with dusting powder so he looked pale and tired. He was waiting in bed when Tiger ran in.

---

[1] A draft horse is used for heavy work.

"Anansi! Anansi!" yelled Tiger. "Come out here and take your punishment like a man!"

"Who's there?" asked Anansi in a weak voice.

"You heard me! Come out now!"

"Please," whispered Anansi. "Please keep your voice down. I don't remember when I've felt so awful."

When Tiger saw him there in the bed, something in his heart was touched. You see, despite his size and strength, Tiger was a decent sort of fellow—the sort who cared about others and tried to be helpful. His anger cooled down, and his voice filled with concern.

"Brother Anansi," he said, "you look pale and quite unwell."

"I've a fever, my friend," said the clever Anansi, "and I fear I'm fading."

"Have you taken any medicine? Have you seen the doctor?"

"My loved ones are away. I've been too weak to get help."

"Then I shall get help for you," volunteered Tiger.

"No!" cried Anansi. "Don't leave me, please. I'm afraid I will die here alone."

"Then what shall I do?"

"You could carry me to the doctor," suggested Anansi.

"Come, my friend," said Tiger, crouching so that Anansi could hop on his back. But just as Tiger stood, Anansi slipped off.

"What is the problem?" asked Tiger, though he wasn't sure he wanted to know.

"I'm afraid your beautiful coat is too soft and smooth to hold on to. Perhaps if we put on a saddle."

"But of course," said Tiger, crouching again so Anansi could saddle him up.

They took off down the street toward the doctor's house. Anansi slapped Tiger's side with a riding crop.[2]

"Ow!" roared Tiger. "What was that for?"

[2] A crop is a small whip used by a horse rider.

"There are so many flies today," said clever Anansi. "I am brushing them away with my whip."

"Thank you, my friend," said Tiger.

Anansi rode Tiger all over town until there was so much sweat in his eyes, Tiger could hardly see.

"Are we there yet?" cried Tiger.

"Turn right here," said Anansi.

Anansi sat up high in the saddle like a jockey and whipped Tiger's side with the crop. Poor Tiger was **exhausted** and could hardly lift his head. He did not know that he had been ridden right up to the lovely young lady's door.

"Good afternoon, ma'am," said Anansi. "A lovely day, is it not?"

The young lady was so charmed by the rider that she invited him in for tea and cookies. And as for Tiger, he was so embarrassed that he ran away and has not been seen in town since.

INSIGHTS

This story is perhaps the most unusual in the collection. It contains a number of features that make it unique. First is the fact that the story contains a tiger. As you are probably aware, there are no tigers in North America, except in zoos. And there were no zoos at the time this story was originally told. So the tiger in the story is one direct link with Africa. But even there, tigers do not exist in every place.

Therefore, this story provides ethnographers (people who study culture) with an interesting puzzle to solve. Was the tale originally told in America by a slave who had come from a region where there were tigers? Perhaps, but it's easy to jump to the wrong conclusion. When the slave traders brought Africans to America, the slaves were purposely separated into groups so that individuals from one tribe would be mixed with those from another. This was done so that the captured people—who spoke a range of different languages—could not communicate and plan a takeover of the ship. So it's possible that the story was invented by a slave from a region with no tigers. The person may have learned about the animals from other slaves on the ship.

Anansi is the other connection this story has to the African continent. But his character in this African American tale is different than his character in tales from Africa. In African tales, we see Anansi as a spider. He is described as climbing and using webs to trap people. But in this story he is not described at all. He is very human in that he visits with others in the community and is apparently just as strong and capable as everyone else.

So what is he? There is no correct answer to this question—your imagination can create an image of Anansi in the way that works best for you. That's one of the features that make storytelling so enjoyable. You can create your own mental pictures as you listen.

TUG OF WAR

VOCABULARY PREVIEW

The following words appear in the story. Review the list
and get to know the words before you read the story.

agile—lively; quick
disguising—dressing; hiding
duped—tricked; fooled
eavesdropping—secretly listening
flare—signal; command
humble—modest; respectful; bashful
lamented—grieved; felt sorrow
leverage—lifting power; strength
mired—sunk; stuck
obnoxious—annoying; unpleasant
perceptive—smart; alert
resistance—obstacle; opposition
ruckus—uproar; fuss
taut—tight; strained; tense
touted—boasted of; bragged about
wretched—miserable; awful

Main Characters

Mrs. Whale—biggest creature in the ocean
Mr. Elephant—biggest creature on land
Mr. Rabbit—trickster

Everyone accepted that the biggest land animal was the elephant and the biggest ocean creature was the whale. Even Mr. Elephant and Mrs. Whale bragged about this fact. One day that sneaky old Rabbit decided to quiet these giants. He even figured out a way to live to tell about it.

TUG OF WAR

There was a running battle among all the animals. Each competed for the titles of tallest, fiercest, strongest, toughest, and most handsome. When two or more animals came together, it wasn't long before the talk turned to which among them was the best. Even the least among them, the flea, **touted** her claim to fame as the quickest and most **agile**. However, they all knew the truth. There was one on the land and another in the sea who could really claim to be the greatest of all. And these two could proudly prove those claims when called to the task. On the land it was Mr. Elephant, and in the sea it was Mrs. Whale.

One could often find the elephant down by the sea visiting his large, wet friend. The elephant trumpeted his accomplishments, and the whale spouted off about her own.

"We are blessed, my sister," said the elephant, waving his trunk high and leaving his large footprints in the damp sand by the sea.

"We are indeed," replied the whale. "The world belongs to us."

"You, my friend, rule the sea," said Mr. Elephant. "And I am master of all who walk on the land. Should any dare to say otherwise, they are itching for a fight from the both of us."

"We'll take on all comers," replied Mrs. Whale, and the two of them laughed, splashed, stomped, and generally created a **ruckus** along the shoreline.

Now it happened that Mr. Rabbit was wandering by about this time. He overheard the discussion between the whale and the elephant. While **eavesdropping**, he wandered close to the water's edge. Suddenly, Mr. Rabbit's favorite vest was spattered by the sand and muck stirred up by the elephant and whale. This was most upsetting because he had worn the lovely vest only a few times.

As we all know, there were two things in the world Mr. Rabbit could not stand. One was a big-mouth braggart, and the other was getting his clothes messed up. On that day, he had the misfortune to be visited by both **wretched** events at the same time. And all because of those two braggarts.

"I'll fix them both!" he vowed, and he set to making a plan to do just that.

First, he searched for the longest and strongest piece of rope he could find. Then, **disguising** himself as a farmer, he sought out the elephant. The great animal was in his usual napping place, down past the coconut grove, just this side of where the river flows into the sea.

"Excuse me, Mr. Elephant," Mr. Rabbit said. "I hear from all who know you that you are the biggest and the strongest in all the land. I'm wondering if I can call on you to help me?" Mr. Rabbit kept his eyes low. He spoke in a **humble** manner to impress the elephant with his respect.

"Certainly," replied the elephant. Mr. Elephant liked nothing better than a compliment. He puffed up with pride—so he was even larger than his already massive size. "Why, thank you, my good man. Anything I can help you with, I would be glad to."

"I knew a person of your strong character and decency would not say no," Mr. Rabbit said, as he bit his lip to keep from laughing. "You see, my cow is stuck in a mud pit just over the hill. You are so powerful and large. If I tie this rope around your leg, you can pull her free."

The elephant positioned himself as asked while Mr. Rabbit tied the rope in a strong knot.

"Wait here, please," said Mr. Rabbit. "When you hear me blow my horn, you may begin pulling."

"As you wish," bowed the elephant, and he sat to wait for the command.

Meanwhile, Mr. Rabbit took off to the shoreline. He travelled just over the hill to the place on the bay that the whale favored most. It was a strip of shoreline bordered with shiny, white grains of sand and palms.

"Excuse me, sister whale," Mr. Rabbit called out. Then he proceeded to run the same story by the whale as he had told the elephant. Except this time he threw in a bit more about beauty and good character.

"Such a **perceptive** young man," observed the whale. "How could I not help you out? Tie your rope around my tail, and I will pull your poor cow free in no time flat."

"Oh, thank you, thank you, oh Large One," cried Mr. Rabbit. "As soon as you hear the blast from my trumpet, you will know my cow is ready to be freed."

With that, Mr. Rabbit bounded up the hill and stood at its top. From there, he could see the elephant on one side and the whale on the other. Both awaited his command. With a great explosion, he blew the signal on his brass horn and pivoted his head back and forth to watch the fun.

At the trumpet's **flare**, the elephant boldly stepped forward.

"Three long strides and I'll have the cow free, even if she's **mired** in concrete." But the back leg to which the rope was tied would not come forward. "She is stuck tighter than I imagined," he said. With that, he began to pull with all of his strength.

On the other end of the rope, now **taut** between the two animals, the whale pulled in the opposite direction. Unlike the elephant, she had no ground to use for **leverage** and found herself being dragged to the shore.

"Oh, no, you don't," said the whale. No cow or any other beast was going to get the better of her. With all her might, she dove toward the bottom of the sea, pulling the elephant behind her as she went.

As we all know, nothing makes an elephant madder than being pulled around. So naturally, Mr. Elephant dug in his heels and mounted a counterattack. Then he pounded back up the beach at a dead run.

Safely hidden in the bushes, Mr. Rabbit watched the two **obnoxious** show-offs foolishly drag each other back and forth. With his advantage of dry land, eventually the elephant dragged the whale to the beach. Once the **resistance** stopped, he ran back to see what he had done.

"YOU!" cried Mr. Elephant. "Why, Rabbit said he needed me to free his cow."

"That's funny," said the whale. "That rascal told me the same thing."

And it was just then they figured out they had both been **duped**.

"Just let him wander near," warned Elephant. "I'll teach him a thing or two about practical jokes."

"That goes double for me," said the whale.

Overhearing this, Mr. Rabbit made a quick run back

into the thick woods where neither Whale nor Elephant could follow.

"Ha! Let them threaten me all they want," he declared. But at the same time, his heart filled with fear. He knew both were strong and powerful. He had to think of a plan that ensured his safety on land and in the sea.

Mr. Rabbit, of course, is never long without a plan of some kind.

In the woods, he came across the body of an old lion who had recently died after a noble life. The lion's once majestic coat was thin and grungy from many years of hard work. This gave the rabbit an idea. He removed the lion's skin and scuffed it up even further so it looked twice as bad. Then he put on the skin and limped down to the sea shore. Once again he found the elephant and whale engaged in their daily brag-fest.

"Brother lion!" cried the whale. "What has happened to you? We knew you were no longer king of the forest, but look what has become of you. You are no more than a gathering of tattered fur."

"Alas, it is that crafty old rabbit," sighed Mr. Rabbit, in his guise as the lion.

"Rabbit!" **lamented** the elephant.

"Yes, I'm afraid it's so. You see, he has powers greater than us all. I know he has put a curse on me for daring to think ill thoughts of him in my sleep."

And with that, Mr. Rabbit hobbled away in his raggedy lion costume.

As you can imagine, the elephant and the whale had a good, long talk after this. They still agreed they were the greatest in the land. But they also agreed that it was best to stay as far away from Mr. Rabbit as they could.

As for Mr. Rabbit, he went on about his business. He smiled to himself whenever he heard the two great creatures boast. "All that strength," said Mr. Rabbit to himself. "Too bad for them I got all the brains!"

INSIGHTS

Mr. Rabbit has been a popular character for as long as African Americans have been telling stories. There are dozens of stories about his adventures, and each story has many different versions that change from teller to teller.

In many of these stories, the small and vulnerable Mr. Rabbit finds himself up against an adversary who is larger, stronger, and usually more conceited than he is. Mr. Rabbit always finds a way to win—often he wins by taking advantage of the other character's high opinion of himself or herself. Because of the way he is always bringing the mighty down, Mr. Rabbit has served as an important hero and role model for African Americans. This was especially true during the time of slavery, when slaves were underdogs in most situations.

Besides his quick mind and ability to understand other characters' weaknesses, Mr. Rabbit has other tools. It's his sharp sense of humor and his ability to laugh even under the hardest of circumstances. And he could often use this as a way to make a fool of the slaveholder. Of course, the slaveholder was never smart enough to see Mr. Rabbit's tricks.

Often in oral tradition, you will see Mr. Rabbit referred to as Brer Rabbit. *Brer* means "brother" and has been used with Rabbit's name for a long time. The person who retells the story can decide how to address the characters. As you tell the stories to your friends and family, you can feel free to choose for yourself which one you prefer.

MR. RABBIT STRIKES AGAIN

VOCABULARY PREVIEW

The following words appear in the story. Review the list and get to know the words before you read the story.

congregate—gather; group
heed—attention; respect
peckish—hungry; starving
prospered—succeeded; gained in status
recount—retell; narrate
scoffed—joked; teased
succumbed—gave in
vicinity—closeness; nearness

Main Characters

Mr. Rabbit—trickster
Mrs. Alligator—mother of twelve

Some creatures will just never be friends. Take rabbits and alligators, for instance. To alligators, rabbits are just not trustworthy. But Mrs. Alligator forgot this unwritten rule and put her trust in Mr. Rabbit. You can be sure she'll never make that mistake again.

Mr. Rabbit Strikes Again

As many of you already know, things have been tense between Mr. Rabbit and the alligators for many a year. There is no need to **recount** that painful story here. Let's just say that the alligators learned their lesson about paying **heed** to that ornery old rabbit. As for Mr. Rabbit, he knew to steer clear of any place the alligators hung out. He knew that should they catch him, a certain family in the swamps would be dining on rabbit stew.

But years had gone by since the feud began, and the alligators had **prospered** and moved to new and better neighborhoods. Mr. Rabbit had become forgetful in his later years and had gone fishing at a lake that he had been fond of in his childhood. He remembered a special fishing place where the big carp liked to **congregate** beneath the overhanging branches of a weeping willow tree.

The shade on this particular day was far out in the water. Rabbit just knew that there were dozens of huge, delicious fish resting in the shaded water. They waited for an afternoon snack of horseflies, who also liked to gather in the shade. Unfortunately, the sun was already well behind Rabbit. And the shady spot with all the fish was just beyond the reach of his pole.

Luckily, there was a log submerged in the water. It angled right out to the shady spot. Mr. Rabbit grabbed his fishing gear, hopped onto the log, and began casting for his dinner.

The fishing was going well. In no time, the rabbit had a long string of whopping big ones. He planned to cook them up that night, along with some spaghetti and corn bread. Just as he felt another bite on his line, he felt the log shift in the water. All at once, the log turned to face him with rows of sharp white teeth. He realized that this was not a log at all.

"You've caught your dinner," Mrs. Alligator said, "and I've caught mine. My kids will be feasting on a nice, fat rabbit."

With those words, she grabbed the rabbit and headed home to serve him to her little ones.

"Please, don't eat me," begged Mr. Rabbit.

The alligator laughed with glee, her teeth shining in the sun like razors. "It will be my pleasure to have you to supper," she said. "After the dirty tricks you've played on my people, you're lucky to have lived this long!"

"But . . . but . . . but . . ." the rabbit stammered, trying to think of a good excuse to give the alligator not to end his life.

"But, nothing," was her reply. "I've got a dozen hungry mouths to feed."

"A dozen mouths?" inquired the rabbit. "Why, I'm barely a mouthful." And suddenly, he had an idea.

"It must be hard raising all those children," he said, shaking his head.

"You have no idea," sighed the alligator. "One wants this, one wants that. A mother's job is never done."

"Today is your lucky day!" cried the rabbit. "It just so happens that you have captured the best baby-sitter in the land."

"You mean the best dinner," **scoffed** the alligator.

"I'm serious, madam," protested Mr. Rabbit. "I am a fine baby-sitter. You'll find that I work hard and that I never let the children out of my sight. With me around, you will be able to go out hunting and go for a stroll. You can even sit in the sun all by yourself and not spend a moment worrying about who's minding the kids."

The rabbit could see from the woman's expression that she was seriously considering his offer. He said one more thing to square the deal.

"Try me out for one day," he said. "If I disappoint you, I'm dinner."

"Okay," said Mrs. Alligator, figuring she had nothing to lose. She carried the rabbit across the log where she and her family made their home. Then she put him to work.

And so the next day, the alligator went about her business, leaving Mr. Rabbit to tend to her family. It was an easy job, really, as alligators are rather lazy. Like their parents, the children mostly liked to lie in the sun or go floating out in the lake. The rabbit leaned back in his chair and enjoyed the sunshine himself. It wasn't the most exciting job in the world, but it was better than being eaten.

A little later in the day, he began feeling a bit **peckish**. It had been a long time since his last meal. He didn't get to eat a single one of those delicious fish he'd strung on the line yesterday afternoon. He looked around and saw that here, where the alligators live, there was not one thing he liked to eat.

Well, there was one thing. Actually, there were twelve things—baby gators.

The baby gators were about bite sized. They did sort of remind him of some of those tough catfish one sometimes pulled up out of the muddy river across the way. But he was awfully hungry. What would it hurt? She had twelve babies. She'd never miss one.

So, while the others were napping, he grabbed one of the babies and ran off to the bushes and gobbled it down in one bite. It was tasty. Better than anything he'd eaten, better than all the fish in all the lakes around.

He couldn't help himself. He grabbed another and snacked that down too. It was just as delicious as the first!

That evening, when Mrs. Alligator came home, she asked how things had been, and Mr. Rabbit reported they all had a wonderful day. The alligator seemed pleased and announced that it was now time for her to bathe her children. They were dirty and covered in mud from playing hard all day long. The rabbit was to bring them to her one at a time.

Mrs. Alligator took her babies from the rabbit one at a time and sang a little song to herself as she dipped them in the water and scrubbed them clean.

In the last light of the sun
I wash baby number one.

And then:

As the leaves fill up with dew,
I wash baby number two.

On she went until she got to ten, and the rabbit began to panic. There were no more babies to bring. What was he to do? He would be tonight's dinner for sure should the alligator discover two of her children were missing.

At the last moment, just as she finished her song, he had a brainstorm that just might work. He ran and grabbed number one, dipped him in mud and dirt again, and carried him back to his mother.

As the stars fill up the heaven,
I clean you, my sweet eleven.

It worked! Apparently Mrs. Alligator was more than a little nearsighted, or maybe all her babies looked the same. But whichever, the rabbit was saved for another day.

The next day went pretty much the same. About the time the sun was straight overhead, those terrible hunger pangs came again. So Mr. Rabbit snacked on a couple of the little ones again. They were as delicious as the meals his mother used to make for special family holidays.

Now, you might think Mr. Rabbit would feel guilty eating up this poor alligator's children. But, you have to remember, there was no love lost between gators and hares. Mr. Rabbit was to have been their dinner too. Turnabout is fair play, as they always say. So he didn't feel guilty. He actually felt rather pleased with himself. He'd found a lovely place to live on a beautiful island. There was fresh food just waiting to be eaten. And he was alive!

And life went on much the same way. Each night Mrs. Alligator would come home and wash her babies and sing to number one . . .

In the last light of the sun
I wash baby number one.

. . . all the way to number twelve:

As the evening shadows creep,
Number twelve must go to sleep.

All the while, Mr. Rabbit ate his way through number nine, and number eight, and number seven, and number six, and number five, and number four, and number two, and finally . . .

Well, finally, after exhausting himself dirtying the same little fellow eleven times and bringing him back to his mother, Mr. Rabbit **succumbed** to his hunger one last time and ate that one as well. He figured he'd better get off that island once and for all. When he thought the coast was clear, he hightailed it out of there and was never seen in the **vicinity** again.

The alligators were, of course, heartbroken. They have sworn to never, *ever* trust a rabbit again. Next time, it'll be dinner time the minute he's caught. There will not even be time for a story, not even a good one like this.

INSIGHTS

In songs you listen to on the radio or jump rope to on the playground, there are almost always words that are repeated over and over again. Sometimes you can't remember all the words to your favorite song, but you can usually remember the parts that are repeated.

If you had a chance to listen to a storyteller from long ago, one thing you would notice is that the stories were full of rhymes, chants, and repeated phrases. When the chant or the repeated phrase was said, often the listeners would say it along with the teller. This technique, referred to by some as "call and response," not only made the stories interesting but also served an important purpose for the storyteller. Often the stories being told were long and complicated. There was a lot for a storyteller to remember. The repeated phrases, rhymes, and chants were tricks that the storyteller used to keep track of his or her place in the story.

The character of the rabbit had its origins in African mythology. It was referred to as the hare. Many other animals saw a transformation as well. For example, the African jackal became the African American fox, and the African tortoise became the African American turtle. The character of the alligator came later in folk history. He was probably a variation of the powerful wolf, sly fox, or stupid bear.

HIGH-FLYING BIRDS

VOCABULARY PREVIEW

The following words appear in the story. Review the list and get to know the words before you read the story.

astounding—surprising; amazing
avail—use; benefit
cacophony—noise; chaos
compelling—persuasive; moving
contempt—disrespect; disgust
contenders—challengers; competitors
crimson—dark red
distinguished—refined; elegant
flitting—moving quickly; darting
impartial—treating all equally; fair
lilting—cheerful; song-like
litany—stories; accounts
recital—telling; report
russet—reddish-brown color
traits—characteristics; qualities
unbiased—fair; open-minded

Main Characters

Mr. Hawk—highest flyer
Ms. Nightingale—clever bird
Mr. Lion—fair judge

Quite a squabble was brewing over who was supreme in the bird kingdom. When the bragging and boasting quieted, it was suggested Mr. Lion decide. So a contest was held, and there was a very unusual winner.

HIGH-FLYING BIRDS

As it happens now and then with all creatures, the birds were getting restless about who among them was supreme. There were **contenders** of every color and size. And each of them had a case more **compelling** than the one before as to why he was more glorious or she more supreme. The owl claimed that she was the one, in that she had been blessed with huge, round eyes. With her vision, she could see even the tiniest creature from miles in the sky.

"It is I!" said the parrot. Then he would proudly spread his **crimson** wings that were tipped with the brightest shades of blue and green. He thought no further words were necessary after such a display. And many who witnessed that demonstration no doubt agreed!

The bragging and boasting went on among the sparrow, the buzzard, the grackle, the ibis, the penguin, and the loon. The thrush, the woodpecker, the robin, the tanager, the dove, the raven, and all their cousins and neighbors also put forth arguments for who was the best and the brightest.

By and by, the arguments became quite heated, and the whole thing threatened to erupt into an enormous mess. Finally, the condors, who are known to be level-headed about most things, proposed a solution. Everyone agreed it was a good one. They decided the disagreement would be taken to a neutral party, who would make a fair and **unbiased** decision. All present pledged that whatever the decision was, they would live with it, even if they didn't like it.

Suddenly, they spotted Lion. He was roaming the field and looking after his land. All agreed there were few as wise and **impartial** as he. Together they approached him and asked him to pick who among them was the greatest of all.

"You ask a tough question, my friends," said Mr. Lion. "How could I begin to choose?"

In answer to his question, the **recital** of achievements began once again. From who had the loveliest eggs to which could sing the sweetest song, each story grew more glorious than the previous. The lion stopped the **litany** midstream.

"Ladies and gentlemen!" he cried. "You are a **distinguished** people indeed. Surely there must be a better way of making your choice."

Just then, who should step forward but the nightingale herself. Now Ms. Nightingale not only had a truly lovely song, but she was also the tiniest among them all. She was so small, in fact, she had been lost among the **cacophony** of louder and seemingly more important voices.

"Excuse me," she chirped, in her **lilting** voice. "I have a suggestion."

"Silence!" roared the lion to the noisy crowd. "Let the young lady speak."

"It seems to me," sang the tiny little bird, "that we have all sung our songs, waved our feathers, and shown off our broods.[1] But we've forgotten what we do best."

"And what might that be?" asked the rooster with **contempt**. These precious little songbirds got on his nerves. What good were they, after all? Did they call the morning sun or manage a whole farmyard? He couldn't see they were much good for anything.

"Well," tweeted Ms. Nightingale, "we can fly."

That shut the rooster up good. Because although chickens had a lot of nice qualities, flying was not among their special **traits**. There was also a lot of booing from some of the other more clumsy birds. The kiwi, who had not been known to take flight at all, was among the loudest. But the complaints were to no **avail**. Like many creatures, the lion was charmed by the nightingale. And he thought she had a terrific idea.

"Of course," he growled, "a flying contest. How perfect. You know, it's the one thing your people can do that I personally envy the most."

And so it was done. There would immediately begin a flying contest among all who chose to enter. Many entered, of course. However, most did it to save face and be good sports. But there was really no contest at all. You see, when it comes to flying, it is well known who the best chap is—it's Mr. Hawk. Some of his close friends, like the eagles, for example, give him a good run for his money. But for the most part, it was the hawk who was destined to be named king.

Still, the birds perched in the trees surrounding the lion's field. Everyone was in a festive mood, eating picnic lunches with their families. No one cared that it was already decided, because it was a lovely afternoon and each was among friends. And nothing was more lovely than birds in flight. It was such a charming day, in fact,

[1] Broods are the babies or young in animal families.

that the birds decided to thank Ms. Nightingale for her idea. But she was nowhere to be seen. That was typical. She was always **flitting** around the sky. She moved so quickly that one would never know where she was at all were it not for her song.

"Brother Hawk," said Lion, saluting him with a bow. "It is now your turn to fly. Should you be the one to fly the highest—and I, for one, have no doubt you will—it will be my honor to name you king of all birds."

Hawk bowed to Lion in return. Then he took his traditional place high in a Norway pine. From there, he soared into the part of the sky that was a brilliant shade of blue only seen by birds. Up he went, past a fluffy white cloud in the shape of a rhinoceros, to a place where the air was thin and clear. His friends on the ground could barely be seen, even with vision as keen as his. He was lost to them as well. He'd gone so far that there was no doubt among any who watched who was the highest flying of them all.

Eventually, Hawk soared toward the ground. He landed in the middle of a vast circle of his peers, right at the feet of the lion.

"**Astounding!**" said Mr. Lion. "I do believe the highest flying creature on earth is in front of my eyes."

"I am flattered . . ." began Mr. Hawk, but he was shushed. The lion extended his paw to just above Hawk's head. Suddenly, a fluttering little **russet** thing emerged from within the feathers on Hawk's head. It settled on Lion's paw. Who should it be but Ms. Nightingale herself.

"Ah, the nightingale. She's a good flyer, a beautiful singer, and a crafty little one on top of everything else!" roared Lion. He turned to the crowd. "I present to you the highest-flying creature of them all!"

The other birds erupted with laughter and applause. Ms. Nightingale bowed and accepted her title.

INSIGHTS

Contest stories are another important part of the African American storytelling tradition. Many tales involve battles between characters to see who is the strongest or bravest of all. "High-Flying Birds" is a good example of a contest story and contains many of the important elements that make such stories enjoyable.

First, contest stories often begin with bragging matches. A group of characters get together and begin exaggerated tales about who is the best. We have all had this experience on the playground or in the lunchroom. As we know, sometimes the only way to solve the problem is to have a contest.

The second feature of contest stories is to find a neutral judge. It is always important to find someone who won't benefit from the outcome—like the lion in this story. It's important that the judge be fair.

The contest in this tale is, more than anything else, a chance for community members to get together and enjoy themselves. People bring their families and friends and have a picnic. This lets us know that the contest is friendly and that everyone, including the contestants, really just wants to have a good time.

Finally, in most contest stories the character that is the likely winner ends up losing. The winner is often the underdog, or the most unlikely contestant of all.

In this story, the small, quiet bird beats the one who everyone knows is supposed to win. These types of contests give the judge great pleasure to be able to settle the bet by awarding the prize to someone who is a complete surprise. And the audience is pleased with the unexpected outcome. They also are reminded that cleverness and determination can take a person a long way.

HOW AND WHY

Mrs. Wind and Mrs. Water:
A Mother's Story

The Old Rooster and Why He Scratches

Stingy Old Mr. Bear and His Grapes

How the Alligator Got His Hide

Why do bears love honey? How did alligators get their rough coats?

Humans have asked questions like these since the beginning of time. And people have often looked to mythology and folktales for answers.

The following stories not only provide interesting answers to these questions. They also reveal the wisdom and humor of the African American people who tell the stories.

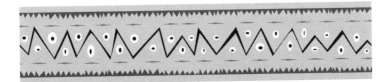

MRS. WIND AND MRS. WATER: A MOTHER'S STORY

VOCABULARY PREVIEW

The following words appear in the story. Review the list and get to know the words before you read the story.

customary—usual; normal
frothing—foaming; bubbling
plaintive—sad; mournful
promoted—moved up; advanced
spiteful—mean; cruel
unceasingly—constantly; always

Main Characters

Mrs. Wind—boastful mother; friend of Mrs. Water
Mrs. Water—boastful mother; friend of Mrs. Wind

Did you ever wonder what caused the whitecaps in the ocean? Well, it's a tragic story that begins with Mrs. Wind and Mrs. Water.

Mrs. Wind and Mrs. Water: A Mother's Story

Now, you've all heard about Mrs. Wind and Mrs. Water. There was a time when they were the best of friends. Often Mrs. Wind would be off doing her job. She would keep the air fresh and the seeds blowing. And Mrs. Water would be busy with her duties. She would sweeten the earth so those same seeds could grow. But when they weren't working, you could often find them together. They had much in common. You see, they each had many children, and, like all mothers, they enjoyed getting together to share stories of what their boys and girls were doing. Mrs. Wind would bring a basket of mending or needlework and sit down by the sea. Then she and Mrs. Water would gossip away the afternoons and enjoy the lovely weather.

"Did I tell you about my oldest girl?" asked Mrs. Water. "She has the best grades in her class!"

"That is nothing," said Mrs. Wind. "Each one of my children has done so well, they have been **promoted** two grades!"

Mrs. Water understood how proud Mrs. Wind was. Why, a mother couldn't help but be proud of her children. She shared with Mrs. Wind the story of her son, who had run faster than anyone and had won a bright blue ribbon the color of the sky.

"My children have won so many ribbons that they stretch around the world," Mrs. Wind responded. She went on to tell how her children were the biggest, the prettiest, the tallest, and the most intelligent. She went on and on until Mrs. Water was afraid she'd never stop.

This conversation went on for many days, with Mrs. Wind always having to say her children were better. Poor Mrs. Water tried to be patient, but she became very angry. Her children were wonderful also. Just because Mrs. Wind was a big braggart and could talk nonstop didn't mean her children were the best around. Mrs. Water grew increasingly angry, so she decided to get even.

One day some of Mrs. Wind's children were out playing near the sea. It was a hot day, and the children were playing hard. By and by, they became very thirsty. They knew that Mrs. Water was a friend of their mother's and thought they would ask her for a cool drink.

"Mrs. Water!" they yelled. "We are thirsty and far from home. Can we trouble you for a cool drink?"

"Of course, children," Mrs. Water replied. "I would be happy to serve you. Please come and make yourselves at home."

When the children moved closer, Mrs. Water grabbed them, pulled them under the water, and trapped them with her. She was satisfied that she wouldn't have to listen to another story about these brats.

Meanwhile, Mrs. Wind became worried about her children, who had been out playing much longer than was

customary. She wandered their usual playgrounds but could not find them anywhere. Eventually, she wandered down by the sea to the home of Mrs. Water.

"Mrs. Water!" she shouted. "Mrs. Water! Have you seen my little ones? They've been gone ever so long."

"No children around here all day," Mrs. Water replied.

But Mrs. Wind didn't believe her. She knew her children had been playing by the sea. So she called to them with a long, **plaintive** howl.

Mrs. Wind's children heard their mother's voice and swam to the surface, trying to escape the sea. But they could not. All Mrs. Wind could see was the white of their feathers brushing against the top of the waves.

"Give them back," Mrs. Wind demanded. Mrs. Water just laughed at her in a joyful, yet **spiteful,** way as she **unceasingly** splashed waves against the shore.

So even now, when you go to the sea, you can hear Mrs. Wind calling for her young ones. You can even see them out there in the ocean trying to get home. They are the whitecaps, **frothing** on top of Mrs. Water, fighting to escape. And there are big storms at sea, when the wind howls and the waves rise high in the air. Don't be afraid; that's just the former friends, Mrs. Wind and Mrs. Water. They will always be fighting over the children that never came home.

INSIGHTS

Have you ever wondered where lightning comes from or why some animals behave the way they do? If so, you're like many of the people who have told stories over time. Some folktales serve the purpose of explaining why the world works the way it does.

People have always been curious about the natural world. Over time, science has come up with theories that explain most of what we observe. However, before we had science, we had stories. The tellers of tales came up with a whole range of interesting, strange, and sometimes humorous ways of explaining the ways things work.

Some stories explain very small, everyday phenomena—like why porcupines curl up or why dogs howl at the moon. Others try to explain big things, such as the reasons the sea sometimes seems to be alive, or why there is day and night. All the stories in the How and Why section are examples of how ancient people tried to understand and deal with their world.

THE OLD ROOSTER AND WHY HE SCRATCHES

VOCABULARY PREVIEW

The following words appear in the story. Review the list and get to know the words before you read the story.

adorned—decorated; filled
cater—provide a meal; furnish food
collective—all together; as a group
delectable—tasty; delicious
flourishing—parading; strutting
furiously—excitedly; rapidly; wildly
gape—stare in surprise
mutters—mumbles; says to oneself
nuisance—pest; pain in the neck
paltry—small; worthless
repast—big meal; feast
scurrying—hurrying; racing
stalked—walked angrily; marched proudly

Main Characters

Rooster—proud fellow
Sister Hen—peacemaker

Poor old Rooster. He spends most of his day scratching the ground and muttering to himself. You might feel sorry for him—until you learn the reason for his strange behavior.

The Old Rooster and Why He Scratches

All the animals had been working hard at their various jobs. So to celebrate, they decided to get together and have a big feast. Since they were too tired to cook, they called their favorite restaurant. It was the only one in town that served foods everyone liked. The owner of the restaurant said that he'd be glad to **cater** the party. In fact, he would create a special dinner that would surprise and delight each and every one.

The feast was held in the town hall that night. When the animals arrived, they couldn't believe their eyes. Each table was **adorned** with steaming mounds of golden food. The animals rushed to their places to inspect the **delectable** food more closely. They oohed and aahed when they realized the golden mounds were actually buttery corn bread, fresh and oven-hot!

"Let's dig in," everyone cried.

Everyone, that is, except Rooster.

Now, Rooster is known about these parts as a tough sort of fellow to get along with. To begin with, he's an early riser. And he feels everyone else should get up when he does. So, while the sheep, the goats, and the rest of the animals are still enjoying their sweet rest, here he comes. And just before the sun stretches its arms into the horizon, Rooster disturbs the peace with his cock-a-doodle-doo.

Sometimes Rooster acts like he owns the barnyard. Why, no one can just innocently stroll through, minding his own business. Rooster is always there, pecking around the person's feet. The rooster makes such a **nuisance** of himself that finally it gets to where decent folks don't want to be around him.

Now, despite all that, the animals had still invited the rooster to the feast. They knew that though he was ornery, he had never been lazy. Still, none of them expected the display of bad manners that Rooster provided.

"What's up with this food?" crowed the rooster.

"You have a problem with it?" asked Sister Hen sincerely. She was known by all to be a peacemaker. So naturally, she would try to keep the evening from being ruined.

"Problem!" crowed the rooster. "Am I the only one here who sees the problem? Look at this food. Why, it's nothing but corn bread!"

"I'm sure you'll find—" started Sister Hen, but the rooster cut her off before she could finish.

"Corn bread here," crowed the rooster, pointing to one table. "And here," he said, pointing to another, "and here. Corn bread as far as the eye can see. I can get plenty of corn bread at home, thank you very much. I'll not stay around for this **paltry** meal."

With that, the rooster **stalked** from the room, **flourishing** his tail feathers behind him. Some of the animals stared after him, **gape** mouthed. However, many of them were pleased that the old complainer had left. All the fussing would be over, and there would be even more food left for those who remained.

Everyone dug in, plucking the still-steaming corn bread from heaping platters. But an even bigger surprise was awaiting the animals. What do you think they found buried under the corn bread? Why, every tasty dish you could imagine, that's what. There was pizza, barbecued ribs, onion rings, cheesecakes, cherry pies, lemon pies, and apple pies. Everyone's favorite dish was hidden under one of the piles of corn bread. The owner of the restaurant had kept his word. He'd made a meal to surprise and delight everyone.

A **collective** cry of joy arose from the animals as they uncovered the secret dishes. The loud cries brought the rooster **scurrying** back to see what he was missing. You see, he was as nosy as he was ornery. When he saw the **repast** that had been uncovered, he sputtered with anger.

"How could I have been fooled by that silly chef?" he asked himself disgustedly. But his pride kept him from rejoining the group, although the other animals surely would not have minded. Instead, old Rooster crept back to his home, missing what was perhaps the best banquet of his life.

Poor Rooster. If only he had learned that things are not always as they appear to be. No one had ever taught him that patience is often rewarded.

That feast did teach the old rooster one lesson, however. The old bird still struts around the barnyard, but if you watch him for awhile, you'll see something else. Every so often, he scratches the ground, digging way down into the dirt. It looks like he's searching for something hidden beneath the soil. And around suppertime, he scratches **furiously,** going after every little grain of corn.

"One of these days I'll find a feast," he **mutters.** "One of these days."

INSIGHTS

Many folktales feature animals having parties. The celebrations always include lots of good food and drink, and everyone has a good time together. But these stories, as all stories, always have a conflict. Sometimes characters are hurt because they are left out of the celebration. Other times the problem is a character who cannot appreciate all the good things that are available. Such stories recognize two important features of African American life.

First is the importance of community celebrations and togetherness. In most places in the South, life was very difficult for blacks. It was important to stick together and to help one another out at all times. It was also important to celebrate the milestones that the community reached. These included births and marriages, a successful crop, or the safe return of someone from a long trip.

Second, these stories also pass along important information. They teach how to make the party a success and how one should behave there. One lesson is to always have enough food. Another is to always be sure everyone is included. Finally, if you're not a gracious host yourself, don't expect to be treated well by others.

STINGY OLD MR. BEAR AND HIS GRAPES

VOCABULARY PREVIEW

The following words appear in the story. Review the list and get to know the words before you read the story.

clambered—crawled awkwardly; scrambled
cultivate—care for; make grow
gloated—bragged; boasted
grudge—mean thought; bitterness
hoard—stock up; save
intimidated—scared; bullied
luscious—tasty; juicy
monumental—important; huge
optimum—maximum; ideal
prowls—searches; roamings
remnants—remains; leftovers
ridiculed—made fun of; mocked
succulent—juicy; delicious
transplanted—replanted; uprooted
vigor—energy; strength
withered—dried up

Main Characters

Mr. Bear—tends a grapevine
Mr. Possum—eats Mr. Bear's grapes

Have you ever wondered why bears are so crazy about honey? It wasn't always that way. Grapes were a bear's first love. Then a hungry little possum came along and changed all that.

STINGY OLD MR. BEAR AND HIS GRAPES

The bear wasn't always crazy for honey. His favorite food used to be grapes, but he gave up on those. This is the story of why that happened.

It seems on one of his **prowls** through the woods, Mr. Bear came across an old, dried-up grapevine. It was late in the year, so only a few **withered** fruits remained on the vine. The rest had been picked clean by the birds, the raccoons, and all the others in that part of the forest. But up high, where only the bear could reach, there were a few sweet **remnants**. They had almost dried into raisins. Mr.

Bear plucked a round, violet beauty and popped it into his mouth. When the tangy, sweet juice burst on his tongue, he knew he had to have more grapes. He **clambered** along the vine and picked every remaining piece of fruit. Still those were not enough.

But Mr. Bear had not seen another vine like this in all his travels through the woods. And he had traveled far and wide. Right then and there he made a **monumental** decision. He would take a piece of the marvelous plant home and **cultivate** it himself. Then the next year he would have a grapevine all his own.

And that was exactly what he did. Mr. Bear **transplanted** the vine to the sunniest part of the hill. Near his den, the plant could attach itself to the fence. He wanted it to put down deep roots and grow strong and healthy.

Now Mr. Bear was a responsible farmer. Some, like his wife, thought him too responsible. He spent night and day in the field looking after the vine. His wife complained that he paid more attention to that grapevine than he did to her.

To everyone's amazement, Mr. Bear's vine grew with great speed and **vigor**. It wasn't long before it was covered with tiny green clusters. This indicated that soon there would be bushel baskets full of grapes.

Things went along smoothly, and the harvest season approached. As the fruit began to ripen to a rich purple, the bear began to remember how **luscious** it really was. He would lie awake at night, remembering the flavor of the sweet juice. He began to wonder if even the plentiful crop he was expecting would be enough for his huge appetite.

His wife, in the meantime, became crankier and crankier. "Since my husband spends so much time with his precious vines," she thought, "there'd better be some fruit for me." So she began to ask for grapes for herself. After all, it wasn't fair of him to **hoard** all that fruit.

But the bear ignored her fussing. The grapes, he had decided, needed to remain on the vine until they were just perfect. They had to have just the right amount of sweetness with an **optimum** number of clusters. It was hard, but he held himself to sampling just one grape here and there. Patiently, he waited for the perfect moment. Then he planned to have a big feast.

About this time, the possum was out searching for his nighttime meal. The sneaky fellow came upon the bear's luscious grapevine. He'd never seen the fruit before, so he reached up and sampled one. As you would expect, he loved it. Quickly he gobbled up all he could reach. Then he set off to clue all his friends in on his tasty discovery.

It wasn't long until the vine was swarming with animals. The rabbits, the raccoons, the foxes, and even the dogs came. Each of them fell in love with the grapes. In that one night, while Mr. Bear slept, the vine was stripped of its **succulent** fruit.

In the morning, when the bear returned to his vineyard, he found that not one grape remained. He growled with anger and grief because he had waited so long for the sweetest pleasure he knew. And now it was all gone. His wife, of course, **gloated** a bit. She **ridiculed** him for having been so selfish and short-sighted. But Mr. Bear quickly forgot all her silly words. His mind turned to revenge. He vowed to find the one who had done him this unforgivable wrong.

Now, keep in mind that the bear is one of the most feared creatures in the woods. So when he set off to find the guilty party, all the animals took notice. He bustled and hustled his way through the brush. Sure enough, it wasn't long before he had **intimidated** some of the lesser creatures into telling what had happened to his crop. To save their own skins, they all pointed their fingers at Possum.

Though Mr. Possum tried to deny everything, the lie was written all over his face. You see, he had stuffed so many grapes into his mouth that his beard was still stained purple. The bear was furious and tried to swat the possum with a large paw. But the possum balled up and made himself hard to see. When the bear turned away, the possum scampered into a thick tangle of bushes. He was sure the bear couldn't get in there.

That first time was also the last time that Mr. Bear tried to grow himself some grapes. He let his vines go wild. For a long time, he was a cranky old thing, and he's cranky to this very day. Nowadays, the bear eats honey to satisfy his sweet tooth. He's the only animal big enough and brave enough to mess around with bees.

So beware if you're out walking and you happen to get between Mr. Bear and the place where the bees store honey. Move aside quickly because that old bear has been carrying a **grudge** for a long time. And he doesn't care whom he takes it out on.

INSIGHTS

Until a few decades ago, Southern African Americans were mostly agricultural people. This means that many of them spent their days growing crops. They grew many kinds of products, such as cotton, tobacco, sugar cane, and vegetables. Any family involved with farming knows that it's hard work and that many things can go wrong. Sometimes a whole season's work can be ruined by a storm, a flood, or lack of rain.

Often black Southerners did not work for themselves. It was difficult for African American families to save enough money to buy their own land. Much of their labor and profit benefited others, both during and after slavery. Most of the crops that free blacks raised had to be given to the person they "rented" their land from. Thus, they were called *sharecroppers* because they had to share their crop with the property owner. But in reality, the landowner generally got all their profits.

Because so many lives revolved around farming in some way, many African American stories also involve growing or getting food. Characters in African American folktales are often worried about how they'll get their next meal or how they can protect their crops. Or worse, they turn their backs, and some clever creature comes along and steals all their hard work. This is what happened to stingy old Mr. Bear. He lost his crop of grapes to clever Mr. Possum.

In the middle of the 20th century, there was a great migration of African Americans to cities in the North. They traveled to places such as Detroit, Chicago, and New York. Job opportunities were opening up due to World War II and the post-war economy. As the people's surroundings changed, so did their stories. Many recent tales deal with the adventures and problems of people in the city.

HOW THE ALLIGATOR GOT HIS HIDE

VOCABULARY PREVIEW

The following words appear in the story. Review the list and get to know the words before you read the story.

escorted—led; guided
irate—very mad; furious
lustrous—shiny; bright
pretensions—false claims; boastings
provider—supporter; caregiver
refined—tasteful; high-class
uncivilized—lacking manners; uncultured
uppity—snobbish; superior

Main Characters

the Gators—snobbish family
Mr. Rabbit—trickster

The Gator family thought they had every-thing. One day Mr. Rabbit came along and introduced them to the one thing they didn't have, and then trouble stepped in.

How the Alligator Got His Hide

The alligator family lived down at the swampy part of the lagoon[1]—Mr. Gator, Mrs. Gator, and the all the little Gator children, that is. For the most part, they kept to themselves. They had everything they needed right there at home, you see. There was plenty of fish to eat and lots of other gators for company. Some people found them stand-offish, but generally folks let them go about their business. They were bright and shiny, like new dimes. And they liked to lie in the sun and show off their beautiful silvery coats. All in all, they were happy and enjoyed life.

[1] A lagoon is a shallow pond typically connected to a larger body of water.

No other animals really talked to the Gators, except Mr. Rabbit. It wasn't that he liked them, because he didn't. He couldn't stand the way they kept to themselves. He hated that they considered themselves better than the others. But Mr. Rabbit talked to everybody, of course. He was such a chatterbox. He would talk to a tree stump if no one else was around.

Mr. Rabbit came across Mr. and Mrs. Gator one day. They were propped up on the riverbank, napping in the warm sun.

"Afternoon, ma'am, sir," said Rabbit.

Mr. Gator propped open one eye to see who had the nerve to disturb his nap. It was only that pesky old rabbit. Eventually, Mr. Gator opened his big jaw and mumbled, "Afternoon to you."

Mr. Rabbit, who feared everyone was losing the fine art of conversation, took offense at this cool response. What did it hurt to exchange a few words with a neighbor? He decided to give them another chance.

"And how's that lovely family of yours?" Mr. Rabbit asked.

Mrs. Gator yawned. Why couldn't these tiresome people leave her and her husband to rest? "If you must know, our children are fine—healthy, smart, well-mannered, and **refined**. And, frankly, I don't know how you land creatures manage without the advantages we have down here at the lake."

The nerve of these Gators, Mr. Rabbit thought. Lying here by the lake all day and then pretending they are better than others. Someone needed to teach the Gators a lesson.

And who better than Mr. Rabbit? But he played it cool. He decided he would go along with their **pretensions**.

"Why, you're right, Mrs. Gator," he said. "Things up here on dry land get pretty tough for us all. The only thing we have that you don't have is lots of trouble."

"Trouble?" asked Mr. Gator. He liked to believe he was the best **provider** in the land. His family had everything they needed and certainly more than all the others around. But what was this trouble? And why didn't his people have any of it?

"Tell me more about this trouble," he ordered Mr. Rabbit.

"I'm shocked, Mr. Gator," said Rabbit. "I can't believe you've never heard of trouble!"

"I have no idea what this trouble is," said Mr. Gator. "But I know that if it's something you dry-land creatures have, then my family and I must have some too."

Great, thought Mr. Rabbit, they may think they're better than the rest of us, but they sure aren't smarter. If they want trouble, I'll find them some. He decided he needed one more layer of temptation before he set his trap.

"I'm not sure, Mr. Gator. When people see trouble for the first time, they usually hope to never see trouble again."

"Nonsense," said Mr. Gator. "The Gator family has the best of everything. This will include the best of trouble from now on. You must show us some trouble at once."

"I'm rather busy."

"Come off it," said Mrs. Gator. "You're a land animal. What could you possibly have to do that's important? Stop stalling and start being neighborly!"

"If you insist," said Mr. Rabbit. "But I'll tell you what. Trouble is better when the whole family is involved. Why don't you meet me here in the morning with all the little ones, and I will take you all to meet trouble in person. How's that?"

"You are a fine friend, Mr. Rabbit," said Mr. Gator. So he and Mrs. Gator made plans to take the whole family on the outing.

In the morning, the Gators woke early to prepare for the big day. They all dressed in their finest coats—they polished them to be extra shiny in the morning sun. Father Gator gathered his brood[1] at the edge of the lagoon and praised them for their fine appearance.

---

[1] A *brood* is a group of babies or young in animal families.

"There's not a more beautiful family in the land than mine!" he bellowed, and all the children beamed with pride.

Soon Mr. Rabbit appeared, himself dressed in his finest furs.

"How marvelous you all look!" he cheered.

"The alligator family always looks divine," said Mrs. Gator.

Rabbit shook with anger inside. He'd fix these **uppity** Gators once and for all. Like the actor he was, he kept his feelings hidden behind a toothy smile. "Come with me, then," he said.

Mr. Gator took his wife's hand and **escorted** the family on their adventure.

Mr. Rabbit led the Gators through the woods to a path through a field of tall, dry grass. The little Gators were so excited about meeting trouble that their voices kept getting louder, and Mrs. Gator had to stop them now and then and ask them to calm down.

"I'll not have folks thinking we're **uncivilized**," she said, brushing some dirt from the feet of one of the youngest.

Mr. Rabbit stopped them in the middle of the large dry field. He cupped his hand to his big ear.

"What did you say?" he yelled. "Did you hear that? Someone is calling me."

"I don't hear a thing," said Mr. Gator, but the rabbit shushed him.

"Listen," Mr. Rabbit said. "Hear? Yes, someone is definitely calling. I must run and see what they need. You all wait right here. Trouble will be along in a minute." Mr. Rabbit scampered away toward the edge of the field.

Mr. Rabbit was so delighted with his plan, he doubled over with laughter. He checked the direction of the wind and took a package of matches from his vest pocket. Next, he gathered a bundle of twigs and lit the end on fire. Circling the field, he set the edge of the tall grass aflame.

"Here comes trouble!" he said with glee. And he climbed to a high, safe mound to watch the action.

Meanwhile, the Gators sat pulsing with excitement, waiting for trouble to arrive. The oldest boy Gator spotted off in the distance a dancing red glow with fog on the top—fog just like down at the lagoon.

"Look, Father," he said. "Look what's coming. Is that trouble?"

"Aha!" said Mr. Gator. "I believe that is trouble!"

"Trouble is pretty," said the oldest girl.

"Look there," said Mrs. Gator. "Trouble is on this side too."

Mr. Gator spun all the way around. "Trouble is everywhere!" he said.

Just then a hot cinder landed on the oldest girl's back. "Ouch!" she cried. "Trouble is hot and trouble hurts."

"Ouch!" cried her brother. Trouble was landing on him too.

"Don't be rude," said their mother. "We must greet our gift with joy." Just then a cinder landed on her. "Yow!" she screamed. "It's true. This trouble is a pain!"

Soon the Gators were surrounded by trouble. Flaming ash landed on their backs like rain. Everyone was shouting with pain.

"Rabbit!" yelled the father. "Call trouble away. Please!" But there was no answer.

When they could no longer stand it, the father gathered his loved ones and led them from the burning field. The flames crackled at their backs as they fled at top speed to the lagoon. Once home, they splashed beneath the waves and let the water soothe their pain. They stayed underwater a long time.

When Mr. Gator popped his head up, there was Mr. Rabbit on the shore. He was rolling with laughter.

"So, Brother Gator, trouble has touched your whole family."

Gator was too **irate** to speak. When his family came to the surface, he gasped with grief. Trouble had turned their lovely silver coats to dull brown. And worst of all, their smooth, **lustrous** shines were crackled and scarred.

"Enough!" Mr. Gator howled. "Enough trouble for a lifetime!"

Mr. Rabbit wandered away laughing.

From that day forward, the Gators have had to wear those same ugly brown coats. No longer do they lie about full of pride, but they do still stay to themselves, snapping rudely at any who should happen by the lagoon. All the other animals stay plenty clear too. Especially Mr. Rabbit.

INSIGHTS

We all know that rabbits, alligators, or any other animals can't really talk. They also don't wear clothes, go to parties, or make the kinds of complicated plans the animals in these stories do. But as long as people have been telling stories, they have given the animals in their tales the same qualities that they give humans. This practice is called *personification*.

There are many reasons why characters in folktales are often animals who act and think like humans. One reason is humor. It's funny to imagine animals behaving like humans—especially if they're making fools of themselves.

Another reason is to avoid the danger of making fun of someone or something with a lot of power. When this is the case, animals are a safe substitute for humans. This was especially true for black slaves in America. A slave could tell stories about smart animals tricking cruel or stupid animals. And the slave's owner wouldn't figure out that the stories were making fun of him.

But, perhaps more than anything, we put animals in our stories because we all enjoy watching the way they behave. It is easy to imagine that animals have personalities and are able to think and feel the same things that we do.

RIGHT AND WRONG

Anansi and the Turtle

Anansi Falls into His Own Trap

Little Old Sparrow
and His Big Old Mouth

Every culture must teach its members right from wrong. Failure to do so would mean chaos and possibly destruction of the culture's values.

One of a culture's most important teaching methods is storytelling. The tales in this section warn listeners about the dangers of deceit and gossip. The wrongdoers usually meet with unfortunate ends—including death. And sometimes to make sure the reader or listener learns a lesson from each story, the narrator states the moral at the close.

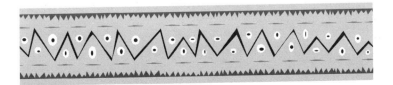

ANANSI AND THE TURTLE

VOCABULARY PREVIEW

The following words appear in the story. Review the list and get to know the words before you read the story.

codger—strange, elderly fellow
courteous—well-mannered; polite
donned—put on; dressed in
fastidious—fussy; very particular
festive—fun; merry
grooming—cleaning up; making oneself neat and attractive
laden—loaded; weighted down
mock—phony; pretend
ornery—mean-spirited; bad-tempered
persnickety—difficult; picky
privilege—pleasure; honor
reciprocate—return in kind; pay back
sincere—from the heart; genuine
threshold—doorway; entrance
trudged—walked slowly; plodded
ungracious—ill-mannered; rude

Main Characters

Anansi—trickster
Mr. Turtle—easygoing turtle

The clever Anansi usually avoided lowly Mr. Turtle. But one day, Anansi accidentally invited Mr. Turtle to a party. Unfortunately for Mr. Turtle, he didn't realize Anansi's rules before he went. Find out how he gets even with Anansi.

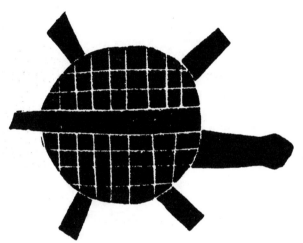

ANANSI AND THE TURTLE

Sometimes there are people we just don't like. This is an unfortunate but well-known fact. Think about our friends Anansi and Mr. Turtle. Mr. Turtle was an easygoing fellow who got along with most everyone. Anansi, however, was a **persnickety** one. When someone rubbed him the wrong way, well, that was pretty much that. If he didn't like you, he wouldn't speak to you or even be around you. Such was his feeling for Mr. Turtle. It wasn't because of anything Mr. Turtle had done. In fact, Mr. Turtle was as fine a gentleman as you'd ever want to meet. He was **courteous** and full of laughter and joy. Anansi just didn't like him. And that was that.

It so happened that Anansi was throwing a party to celebrate the coming of spring. He wanted the party to be big and **festive**. So he made a general invitation to all who lived in those parts.

"Come one, come all!" Anansi announced, and he set about to arrange plenty of food and beverages for everyone. He was headed home with a load of party favors when he happened upon Mr. Turtle, who was out for an afternoon stroll.

"Brother Anansi!" called Turtle. "It is so kind of you to invite me to your party. And, may I say, quite an unexpected surprise as well. I'm looking forward to becoming your friend. May I lend you a hand with your heavy load?"

Drat! thought Anansi as he stood there speechless. He had forgotten when he issued his general invitation that "everyone" included raggedy old Turtle. What was he to do?

Perhaps he should uninvite the fool. He could tell Turtle to stay in his own neighborhood and leave decent folks alone. But that wouldn't do at all. It would be **ungracious** and rude. People would think badly of him. He had to think of a way to trick the turtle and keep him away from the party. So he smiled and thanked Mr. Turtle for the kind offer of help.

"It will be my **privilege** to welcome you to my home tomorrow night," Anansi said with a big smile on his lips. For a moment, he almost seemed **sincere**.

"The pleasure will be all mine," said Mr. Turtle. Then he rushed (or rushed as much as a turtle is able to rush) home to select the perfect outfit for the special occasion.

Meanwhile, Anansi thought of a clever plan. He

announced that new carpet had just been installed in his home. Because of this, all animals who wished to attend his party must wash their hands before entering. Well, this certainly seemed reasonable—more than reasonable to the **fastidious** ones like the cat and the robin. They always spent extra time **grooming** to be sure to look their best.

And so the next afternoon, all the animals cleaned up and began gathering at Anansi's home. All except poor Mr. Turtle, who just couldn't stay clean. He would wash his hands so carefully. But every time he set off for Brother Anansi's, he would immediately find that his hands were just as dirty as before. In frustration, he finally plodded over to his new friend's home. All the washing had made him very hungry. So he was ready to feast on the many delicious foods that he imagined would be there.

"Hand check!" called Anansi as the last few guests crossed the **threshold** to his home. Mr. Turtle just happened to be one of those guests. Each animal raised a freshly scrubbed paw or hoof or foot—all except one.

"Hand check!" called Anansi to Mr. Turtle. But all Mr. Turtle could do was look down in shame at his mud-caked and dust-clogged toes.

"Brother Anansi!" cried the turtle. "You know that I must walk close to the ground. It is impossible to keep my toes clean from one step to the next."

"Sorry," sighed Anansi, "but a rule is a rule." He shook his head, clucked his tongue in **mock** sympathy, and closed the door in the turtle's face.

As he **trudged** back to his home at the lake, Turtle could hear the party behind him. Everyone in town was laughing and drinking and having a wonderful time. He felt sad. Then he started to get mad.

"That **ornery** old Anansi," he grumbled. "He did this on purpose to leave me out!"

With that thought, Mr. Turtle began his own plan to get even with Anansi. He planned a feast at his special place at the bottom of the lake. Like Anansi, he invited the whole town. He went out of his way to stop by and personally invite Anansi.

"I must **reciprocate** your kindness and invite you to my home for a special evening," said Mr. Turtle. "Please say you'll come."

Believe it or not, Anansi was thrilled to be invited. Even though he didn't personally like the turtle, Anansi loved parties. He figured that with all the people there, he would find someone he liked to talk with.

"I'd love to come!" he cheered. "Just tell me the time and the place."

"It'll be at the bottom of the lake on Saturday at two. I'm so pleased you can come," said Turtle as he wandered away.

"The bottom of the lake!" Anansi said to himself. That old **codger**! Everyone knew that Anansi was too light to stay on the bottom of the lake. He always floated to the top. This was a trick—a dirty trick to pay Anansi back for throwing Turtle out of his own party. Well, he'd just see who was the tricky one around here.

On Saturday, Anansi **donned** a disguise of dark glasses and a coat. He wore the coat so he could fill its large, deep pockets with stones. This would keep him submerged at the bottom of the lake with the others who were enjoying the party.

Mr. Turtle was not the fool that Anansi thought. When he saw the strange-looking creature floating to the bottom of the lake, he knew right away who it was.

Turtle warmly greeted each guest as he or she arrived. Then he announced, "My friends, it is a custom here at the bottom of the lake for guests to hang their coats as they enter. Leave them by the pink marble rock and make yourselves at home."

Of course, Anansi knew what would happen if he removed his coat. So he wandered into the party and approached a table that was **laden** with delicious foods and tasty things to drink.

"Excuse me, friend," said Mr. Turtle. "You must remove your coat. You made the rules at your party. I have made them at mine." Then Turtle bowed graciously and watched as Anansi, without his rock-filled coat, floated helplessly to the top of the lake. Not one crumb of the delicious meal did he get to eat.

The soaked Anansi shuffled back to his home. There he had a simple supper with someone he liked—himself.

INSIGHTS

This tale, "Anansi and the Turtle," is an example of a story that seeks to give the listener examples of right behavior and wrong behavior. Stories that serve this purpose are an important part of the storytelling tradition in all cultures. These stories act as a way to pass on important beliefs and values.

This story teaches its lesson in an unusual and interesting way. Many stories present a clear-cut case where one character is only good and the other is only bad. However, this story presents two characters who both make poor choices.

Anansi is a bad friend and neighbor who makes it impossible for Mr. Turtle to attend his party. Anansi is not outwardly mean, but he does construct an obstacle that his neighbor cannot overcome.

But Mr. Turtle isn't a good neighbor either. He wants to get even with Anansi. So he treats Anansi the same way Anansi treated him. While the story teaches the consequences of being a bad neighbor, it also sends another message. It says that if you mistreat others as they mistreat you, bad things can happen. Just as in life, folktales don't always have happy endings.

ANANSI FALLS INTO HIS OWN TRAP

VOCABULARY PREVIEW

The following words appear in the story. Review the list and get to know the words before you read the story.

benevolent—kind; good
enraged—highly angered; worked up
incantation—magic spell; hex
keeled—dropped; fell
perplexed—puzzled; confused
scam—trick; plan to cheat someone
seethed—got worked up

Main Characters

Anansi—trickster
Sister Guinea Hen—wise woman

ANANSI FALLS INTO HIS OWN TRAP

Anansi, as you know, was usually a clever one, but sometimes he was too clever for his own good.

One time he lived in a kingdom where there was a magical queen. She was a **benevolent** ruler, but one thing made her crazy. It seems she had a secret name that she could not bear to hear. Because when she did hear it, she became **enraged** and did foolish things. So naturally, she forbade anyone to say her secret name. If someone did, she'd cast a spell with her magic powers. This **incantation** caused the speaker to drop over dead on the spot.

But clever Anansi discovered the queen's secret name—*Five*. And that wasn't all. He cooked up a plan to get himself an easy meal any time he wished. Here's how he did it.

He pulled his favorite marbles from his bag and wandered down to the water's edge where he knew that many of the animals came daily for a cool drink.

"Excuse me," he said to the mouse. "It seems I've forgotten my glasses. Can you tell me how many marbles I've got here?"

"Well, let's see," said the mouse, trying to be neighborly and helpful. "I see one, two, three, four, five!" And with that, the unfortunate mouse **keeled** over dead. Anansi made a quick and delicious meal of him right there.

Next, along came a poor chickadee. Also a kind soul, she found herself victim of the same **scam**. Unsuspectingly, she became Anansi's midmorning snack.

Things went on this way for awhile. Anansi grew big and fat. He continued to eat his way through each day. But, as always happens, word about Anansi's scam got around.

One sunny afternoon, Sister Guinea Hen—who was just as clever as our friend—wandered to the water's edge. There she discovered old Anansi lying back on the beach with a toothpick dangling from his greasy lips.

"Who goes there?" he cried, his voice dripping with helplessness.

"It is only me, Brother Anansi," cried Sister Guinea Hen. "Look at the lovely eggs you've laid on the beach!" With that, she ran and sat on a shiny, blue marble that was swirled with streaks of red and white.

"Ha!" Anansi laughed. "The old girl is as blind as I pretend to be," he said to himself. "I'll show her a thing or two!"

"Good to see you this fine afternoon," he said. "Can you help me with something? It seems I've misplaced my glasses, and I'm wondering whether you can tell me how many of my marbles remain." And he licked his lips in preparation for a tasty afternoon snack.

"With pleasure!" exclaimed the guinea hen. "I see one, two, three, four, and . . ."—she drew out the count for maximum effect—" . . . and the one I am sitting on." With that, she perched herself on top of the fifth egg.

Anansi was speechless with shock. Here he had prepared for another meal, and he was faced with a stupid woman who could not even count. "Could you do that again, please? I think there must be some mistake."

"Of course," replied the hen. "Let's see. There is one, two, three, four, and then the one I am still sitting on."

"Aargh!" cried Anansi. "Where did you learn to count? That is not even close to being right. Once again, you fool."

Sister Guinea Hen rose up and stood beside the eggs. "One, two, three, four, and this one here," she said, in a **perplexed** voice.

Anansi **seethed** and sucked in through his teeth. "I am losing patience with you. How many is that? How many are here?"

"I don't understand," cried Sister Guinea Hen. "What do you mean?"

"I want to know how many," screamed Anansi. "You counted yourself and there are five!"

In his rage, he had said *five*, and of course he fell over dead. Sister Guinea Hen plucked him up and had a delicious meal. She hobbled on back to the village, happy and full.

As for playing this trick on others, well, that didn't happen with this wise old bird. She had seen firsthand what comes from being too greedy.

INSIGHTS

Folktales are stories of common people and their everyday lives. They are stories told over and over again, from one generation to another. Through the characters and their actions, the tales reflect the history, way of life, values, and humor of a particular culture.

Folktales are a combination of several types of stories. Some began as myths or religious stories. Others resemble fables that use animals to teach morals or lessons. And some are based on legends about real-life people.

Legends are another kind of stories that make their way into folktales. Legends are often based on individuals who actually lived at some point. The stories memorialize their adventures and great deeds. One well-known African American legend is that of John Henry, who was said to be the most powerful man who ever worked on the railroads. His job was to drive the stakes into the ground that are used to hold the tracks in place, and the legend says that he could outwork any man on earth.

Anansi is usually a trickster in African American folktales. He is also an important figure in African mythology. Often Anansi stories use examples of the correct ways to behave. As he tricks or is tricked by others, the listener learns how to treat others.

Tricksters are common to many folk traditions. For example, in the Native American folk culture, the trickster is represented by a coyote. Tricksters use their wit and cleverness to their own advantage. Sometimes tricksters use their skill for good purposes. For example, they may make fun of fools or help others. And sometimes tricksters use their tricks for their own selfish aims. "Anansi Falls into His Own Trap" is an example of a clever creature who, because of his own evil and greed, suffers at the hands of an even wiser animal.

LITTLE OLD SPARROW AND HIS BIG OLD MOUTH

VOCABULARY PREVIEW

The following words appear in the story. Review the list and get to know the words before you read the story.

agitated—worked up; nervous
confront—stand up to; face; deal with
converse—chat; communicate
distract—entertain; sidetrack
eavesdropper—snooper; secret listener
kin—family; relatives
lighted—landed; descended
meddlesome—snoopy; bothersome
mongering—spreading; pushing
nestled—huddled; curled up
rational—reasonable; levelheaded
riled—shaken; stirred
scheming—cooking up; plotting
snit—angry or worked up mood
stewed—worried; fussed
wily—tricky; sly

Main Characters

Mr. Sparrow—troublesome gossip
Mr. Rabbit—busy schemer
Mr. Fox—tricky braggart

Mr. Sparrow was a gossip, no doubt about that! In fact, he was so eager to spread rumors that he didn't recognize a dangerous trap. The foolish bird paid a big price for his big mouth.

Little Old Sparrow and His Big Old Mouth

Now, Mr. Rabbit always bragged about what he was going to do. Most any day, you could find him wandering down some dusty road. He often mumbled to himself about how he was going to teach this one a lesson or make that one pay. But most folks knew that when Mr. Rabbit was just running his mouth, the best thing to do was ignore him. He was all talk most of the time. And if he wasn't, what concern was it of yours?

On this particular day, Mr. Rabbit made his usual rounds. Early that morning he decided to be in a **snit** about Mr. Fox. Who knows what set it off? It could have been that expensive new cologne Mr. Fox was wearing. Or maybe it was Thursday, and Thursday was Mr. Rabbit's day to be mad at Mr. Fox. The reason doesn't matter. All that matters is that Mr. Rabbit was mumbling about the showdown to come.

"I'm gonna fix that fox today," he said. "I'm tired of him bragging about how he's the best in town. I've got a plan to fix him real good. When I'm done, nobody around here will associate with him or any of his **kin.**"

As Mr. Rabbit rambled on and on about his plan, he passed nosy old Mr. Sparrow **nestled** high in a tree. Old Mr. Sparrow and his big nose—or beak in this case—were taking note of every word. But Mr. Rabbit was too busy **scheming** to pay any attention to who might be spying on him.

"Ooooh!" cried Mr. Sparrow. "You bad. And I'm telling. Telling, telling, telling! I can't wait till I see Mr. Fox. I'm fixing you good. Telling!"

"You!" shouted Mr. Rabbit. "Why, you nosy old **eavesdropper.** What business do you have listening in on folks' private conversations?"

"Ha!" laughed the sparrow. "Who are you kidding? In the first place, this is a public area. Any talk here is merely for those who are dumb enough to put their business out in the streets. Second, as far as the conversation part is concerned, it takes two to **converse.** Since I'm the only other person around, I assume you must have been conversing with me. So there! Ha!"

"Why you . . ." threatened Mr. Rabbit. But he didn't get a chance to finish that threat.

"Hold that thought," said Mr. Sparrow as he flew away. "I've got important messages to deliver."

Mr. Rabbit **stewed** for a while, but then he forgot about it. Everyone knew about Mr. Sparrow. He flitted around the woods from tree to tree and always looked to get in someone's personal business. Why, by now, Mr. Sparrow had probably come across some other poor victim on the road. So he probably had someone else's stories to **distract** him.

However, today Mr. Sparrow wasn't distracted. He did find Mr. Fox, and Mr. Sparrow did tell him what Mr. Rabbit said about him. And that, as you can imagine, put Mr. Fox into quite an **agitated** state. You see, all the